The Northwest Passage

By the same author:

The Northwest Passage

A Novel by

NORMAN LAVERS

Fiction Collective New York

FIRST EDITION.

Library of Congress Cataloging-in-Publication Data

Lavers, Norman.
  The Northwest Passage.

  1. Northwest Passage—Fiction. I. Title.
PS3562.A8484N6 1984   813'.54   83-27484
ISBN 0-914590-86-3
ISBN 0-914590-87-1 (pbk.)

Portions of this novel have appeared in slightly different form in *Jeopardy*, *TriQuarterly 42*, *Selected Short Stories by Norman Lavers* (LaCrosse: Juniper Press, 1979), and *Writers Introduce Writers*, ed. Richie & Claire (New York: Groundwater Press, 1980).

Published by the Fiction Collective with assistance from the National Endowment for the Arts and the New York State Council on the Arts, and with the cooperation of Brooklyn College, Teachers & Writers Collaborative, and Illinois State University.

Typeset by Open Studio, Ltd., in Rhinebeck, New York, a non-profit facility for writers, artists and independent literary publishers, supported in part by grants from the New York State Council on the Arts.

Manufactured in the United States of America.

Text & cover design: McPherson & Company
Cover drawing: Cheryl Lavers
Author photograph: Cheryl Lavers

For Cheryl and Gawain

INTRO

JUST IN TIME TO CAP MI LONG-TIME CAREER AS THINK/TEACH JUST WHEN ALL PAPERS OF ANI KIND THOT ALREDDI EDIT/ COLLATE/MIKE TAPE   JUST NOW NE PACIF QUAD IS OPEN UP FOR EXPLORE (NUKE PEACE CLICK COUNT NOW DOWN TO SAFE PARAMETER)   MANI NEW PAPERS RAIN/POUR DOWN ON WE

BECUZ MI BAG IS LIT/LANG I GET ASSINE THIS NEVER PUBLISH BEFOR MS   BUT THEN (LAFF) MAIBE NOT EVER TO BE PUBLISH BECUZ CONTENT NOT SO HOT BUT NOW VERI GUD TO SHOW 2 LEVEL OF THEN/LANG BECUZ (AN THIS VERY GUD IRONI) THIS MS BI A THEN/TIME MAN WHO EDIT EVEN MORE THEN/TIME MS

THIS GIVE ME CHANCE TO STUDI 20 CENT THEN/LANG NEXT TO 18 CENT THEN/LANG NEXT TO OF COURSE WE'S NOW/LANG

ALTHO I PRESENTLI 44 (ALREDDI 1 YR PAST VOLUNTARI- GOODBI) I GIVE MISELF 1 MORE YR EXTEND TO FINISH THIS MI BEST WORK

WHEN 1st EXPLORE/MAN GOED INTO N E PACIF QUAD HE FINDED VERI MANI THEN/STILE APT STILL STAND NOT TO MUCH BREAK BECUZ MOSTLI HI PEACE CLICKS KILL EVERY- THING

EVEN A KIND OF GERM ("an ant" IN THEN/LANG) FOUND TO LIVE THERE (NOW PERSERVE IN CHEM FOR WE'S ECO/THINKS TO STUDI)

N E PACIF QUAD ALREDDI CLEAR/CLEAN FOR DEVELOP/REPOP BUT THIS MS AN OTHERS MI CO-THINKS PRESENTLI EDIT/ COLLATE/MIKE-TAPE LEAVE WE VALUABLE HERITAGE TO MIND LIFE/STILE OF THEN/MAN SO THAT HISTORI BE UP TO DATE NO GAPS

HOPEFULLI MI NOTES AN GLOSS AT BACK WILL HELP HI (AN
BRAVE MID?) LEVEL STUD TO READ THIS MS IN ORIGINAL
THEN/LANG

I PRESENTLI PERPARE COMPUTOR-GLOSS OF EVER WORD INTO
NOW/LANG TO BE USE FOR STUDI AID

INTRODUCTION

ON THE FIRST OF SEPTEMBER, in an evil hour (namely, two minutes to midnight, as I swore to myself that on this day, following a wasted and non-productive summer, I would at least set down the first word of this work, and got up at six am for that purpose, and sat chained in my room, pacing up and down, glaring at the typewriter, a beautiful day outside, no doubt a profusion of rare and previously unrecorded migratory shore birds coming in with the tide on the mudflat out front, till, as you can see, two minutes away from its being the next day, and have here, thank God, finally begun) I commence this undertaking which, even if it were publishable and I could get through it, certainly will not make me three cents, and probably won't help me to get a job anywhere. Anyway, what I am setting out to do, with no prior experience, is to edit this MS which we found in the basement of the county museum when we were moving all the bird skins out to get ready for the renovation. I thought it looked pretty interesting, and since I am the "writer" and the "teacher" and the "historian" and thought I could work out the old handwriting, they turned it over to me, or rather, I grabbed it, so I could make a copy of it, and, if I thought it was worth it, prepare an "edition" of it, which maybe the museum could get a grant to publish on its little photo offset press, maybe my wife doing some illustrations for it.

It's interesting enough. If it's genuine, and it certainly looks it, it might be a major collection of travel journals from one of the early explorers of the Pacific Ocean. Unfortunately Mrs. Thorndike (appallingly accurate name), museum directress, is having second thoughts about it, and thinks if they get the grant maybe *she* ought to edit it and I can just do the dog work of transcribing it for her. I extend her a courteous invitation (seconded by everyone else connected with the museum) to go fuck herself.

Anyway, the MS itself was found under pretty romantic circumstances. An old sourdough up by Old Crow in the Yukon Territory opened up an ice cave in which was a woolly mammoth (such as he—the old sourdough—had often found, and feasted on, and preserved parts of the tusks of to practice his scrimshaw upon) frozen in perfect preservation, and with it the bodies of the last two explorers, who had somehow got into the cave and holed up there and fed on the mammoth, evidently, until they died (not from the mammoth, but, as an autopsy showed, from trichinosis, probably from eating polar bear meat). Before reporting the bodies, the sourdough had appropriated for himself anything among their effects which he thought he could use, this being only a good knife (he didn't know how to use their "foreign"—i.e. flint-lock—rifles) and all their papers, which he took to use for fire lighting and another, even humbler, purpose.

When the U. of British Columbia people said they guessed the bodies were from the ill-fated Montague expedition, which was looking for a northwest passage back in the early 18th century even before Cook, and the hulk of whose crushed ship is still a landmark up by Cape Bathurst (since nothing ever rots up there), he fortunately decided to save what was left of the papers, and brought them with him when he came down here to Washington to end his days at his daughter's house. When he died, she gave them, and some bits of mammoth tusk which he had carved, to the museum, and they had all gone into a box in the basement.

The papers are in several hands, each of which I was soon able to recognize, which was a help in arranging them. Some of the hands are quite clear (once you get on to the weird spelling and the long s's), and some are just about undecipherable. Several sheets were together as they had been written, but others were scattered, and pretty difficult to get back into proper order, since they weren't always paginated or dated. The cold arctic air had preserved them very well, only they had a bit of mildew on them from being stored in his daughter's attic or maybe even the museum basement.

[4]

In transcribing them, I have thought it best to leave the original spelling and punctuation, since I thought it was charming, and gave the flavor of the writing better, and also because it always pissed me off when editors of old books "modernized" them for my benefit, as if I were too dumb to work it out without their help. After a bit of soul-searching, however, I did cop out on the long s's, since I don't have a long s key on my typewriter, and I know the museum would never publish it with long s's. But that's the *only* concession I will tolerate.

Mostly the MS speaks for itself, so I haven't put a lot of footnotes to clarify things, and I'm pretty lazy about doing research, so I didn't trace down references, etc. If some stray name is mentioned, I can't imagine that anyone would really care to have me track him down as, say, "London ship's chandler, b. 1689 at Staithes, Yorks., died ca. 1740 in London, poss. of injuries suffered in a tavern knife fight." However, since the old trapper, probably shitting pretty regularly on sourdough flapjacks (they actually take the sourdough starter to bed with them every night, to keep it alive) used up quite a bit of the MS, or else there wasn't all that much to begin with, in order to make a volume big enough to be book length I have felt free to insert my own comments when they have occurred to me, and to fill in some of the gaps with musings and writings of my own, and about my own life, which I think complement and amplify things that the explorers themselves say.

THE JOURNALS AND LOGS OF
THE ILL-FATED MONTAGUE EXPEDITION
IN SEARCH OF A NORTHWEST PASSAGE, 1749-1751

Transcribed and Edited by
George Herbert

[The first coherent and consecutive entries begin September 14, 1749, as Captain Montague, or Mountague as they spelled it, came up on the Galapagos from the south-east, probably after having coasted up the length of South America on the trades. They had left Plymouth on April 1, 1749, in the *Venture*, with 80 men, and had met an English ship in the Straits of Magellan at the end of July, which is the last they were ever heard from, until 1915, when the broken hulk of the *Venture* was found near Cape Bathurst. So these notes fill in the gaps in the story. (Maybe just on this first entry, to give you the feel of it, I will write the long s's as f's, which are not quite the same, but will give the idea.) Here is, first of all, the captain's journal. He is not much of a writer, nor do his interests seem to extend beyond the quality of anchorage at various stops, and how much money can be made off whatever is discovered at each stop.]

On the 14th Day we came up wt the Iflands *Gallapago's*. We was fteering a coarfe Weft, within 40 Minutes of the *Equator*. The Wind was light, at S. by E., & Iflands appar'd on our Weather-bow, & Lee-bow; & others ftraight on. We made for the Eafter-moft, & anchor'd, abt. Mid-night, in fixteen Fathom Water, in clean, white hard fand.

* * *

He woke up J crawling into bed, and told her he had started the book. She gave him a big hug and kiss, but then went right back to sleep. In the morning while he ate his mush he let her read what he had done so far.

[6]

"It's good," she said (her British accent was still strong, even after six years), "But you'll have to cut out all the shits and fucks for Mrs. Thorndike, and then you'll have to cut out Mrs. Thorndike, too, if you really want to publish it."

"What do you know about art?" he shouted, chasing her out of the kitchen goosing her. She jumped straight into bed surrendering, but though he jumped on top of her and put his arms around her he was already thinking about transcribing more of the manuscript and putting it in place.

"The thing is," he said, "I have to put it down my way to start with, because my real interest is in learning from it, in finding all the correspondences somehow with my life. That's what keeps my interest up. After it's done, I can cut out all the personal parts."

"Will the personal parts have parts about us in it?"

"Maybe."

"You could write a fantastic pornographic novel just about us."

"Yeah," he said absently.

" 'Then she pulled up her nighty, then he put his hand on her cunt—' "

"That's not even good pornography," he said, getting up. "Fix me a cup of coffe so I can get to work."

"You lazy fuck," she said, pulling her nighty back down. She started laughing.

"What?"

"The long s's made me think of when we were home last time and you got that facsimile copy of *The Natural History of Selborne*, and Daddy was reading it aloud, forgetting and pronouncing all the long s's as f's, and unfortunately it was the section about goatsuckers. Mum and I were practically wetting ourselves laughing."

He came back to the bed and started to push her down.

"No you don't. You've missed your chance. Get to work, and now you're going to have to be distracted all day thinking about my luscious body, and if you're *very* lucky, maybe you'll get another chance at it tonight."

* * *

[Here is David Jenkins, the ship's naturalist, already by this time a common feature of ships engaged in scientific exploration. He is, fortunately, a much more copious writer than Captain Montague.]

Sept: 15. We anchor'd in the Night abt. 1 Mile on the East-side of *Chatham* Is. From the Deck then I descri'd the Shape of its *Volcanoes*; pale & Ash-like agaynst the dark Water & Star pouder'd Skie.[1] Now at Dawn I saw it agayne, & the Aspeckt had revers'd, for the Sky & Sea was pale, & the Isle Black as a *Coal* Tipp, & fully as inviting. Despeight the discourageing Apparance, I eagerlie went off in the *Pinace* wth some of the *Boys* going ashoare for Water & Fewell & Food; Dr. *Harris*, accompani'd me.

The Water was dimpl'd with a moderate Breaze out of the S. Few Sea Birds was about, & the Isl. appar'd still & Deathly.

We made our waye Inland thro' a flinty & Cinder heapt Chaos of black *Lava*, like the Rubbel of a grate Iron Works. The Ground acktually clinckt under our Boots. Scrawny Weed-like poor scraps of Vegetation had seiz'd Foothold in crooks & Crannies. However, as we rose in Elevation, the Terrayne relented a Bit. We came thro' a Forrest of small *Incense* Trees, bare of Leaves at this Season, & whistling eerily from the steady *Traydes*, but Aromatick to the Smell when I broak off Twiggs & held them to my Nose. The Sun was beginning to climb, but in the refreshing Breaze not Unpleasant, & now ther was much more Life abowte us, *Lizzards* skuttling across the *Lava* & *Pumice* chasing

[1]THIS APPARENTLI TRU MANI THEN/TIME REPORT EVEN PICS SHOW STARS CUD BE SEE FROM EARTH BECUZ OF NEGATIV AMOUNT OF PARTICULS IN AIR ALSO (THEN/TIME BOOKS SHO) DAITIME SKI BLU INSTED OF NOW'S BROWN

[8]

the abundant small *Locusts*, wch made a constant skittering ahead of us & several *Mocking-Thrushes* & small *Doves*, & nos. of very drabb little blackish *Finches*. Dusky *Buzzards* sat up on Rock Points, or soar'd easily above us, sometimes amazing us wth theire sudden Agility in the Wind Currents, flashing off for the meer Pleasure, twisting & turning like *Faulcons*. But most amazing was the grate Tameness of all the Creaturs, as if too far from the News of the FALL OF MAN to realize that the old PEACABLE KINGDOME no longer obtained. & this to theire Cost, for the *Boys* commenct striking down the *Doves* with Switches, for they was too confiding to flie, even when they saw theire *Fellows* kill'd right next to em.

Dr. *Harris*, & I, continu'd Inland, colleckting Examples of such scraggy *Plants* as we encounterd, with ne'er a *Flower* of any Apparance amongst em, & we droppt into a Valley, or rather Cauldern of fallen-in Crater, making our waye thro' a scrubby Thicket of *Euphorbias* & odd aborescent *Cacti*, & suddenly chaunct upon a Relict of the World before the *Flood*!

Dusky & Clanking antidiluvian *Monsters*, Gigantick black Lumps as if scarcely animated Mounds of the basaltic *Lava* in the very Process of becoming *Life*, lay Soaking in the Oaze & Mud at the Crater Bottom, & were just then haling themselves out, & starting theire many Paths outward no doubt to Forage. High rounded *Carapaces* of Black, sparsley o'ergrown with sooty Moss; scaled & peeling Elephantine Clubb Feet; long swinging Serpent Necks, toppt by tiny comickal *imbecile* old Man Heads. These were the wonderful *Gallapago's* themselves, eponymic Masters of the Serpent *Kingdome* we had enterd, the Giant *Tortoises* we had read of so often in the works of the *Buccaners* of the last Century, who had made to these Isolated Shoares to Careen & New Stock theire *Shipps* in safety from the Eys of the *Mayne*.

Dr. *Harris*, & I, had grate Sport wth these lumbring innocent Creaturs, who scarcely seemed conscious of our Presence intill we was direckly befor em, when they indrew their Hedds with a surpriz'd *Hiss*, clapt theire Leggs to, & clumpt to the Ground.

[9]

Theire Backs was as solid to the toutch as the Bowlders they so much resembl'd, so that when we scrambl'd upon theire Backs, they easily rose to theire Feet & went lumbring on as if we was no weiht at all.

We realizd now that the well beaten *Path* we had followd up from the Beach was made by these Creaturs themselves, & theire *Trayls* radiated from this Spot to all Parts of the arid Lowlands, giving em access to this muddy Pool where they was wont to wallow & drink. Many, in fackt, had theire Hedds clear under the Water, & was drinking copiously, no dou't provisioning theire Bellies like *Camels* befoare setting out on the *Sahara* of theire Island.

The most was 3 or 4 ft. Long, & surely weih'd 3 or 4 cwt. Dr. *Harris*, & I, after a carefull Census, counted 87 of em. We had colleckted, by now, examples of all the *Plants*, & very drabb & unimpressive they were, & the rather few *Invertibrates* — 3 Kinds of *Arachnid*, a *Bee*, a *Butterflie*, 3 Kinds of *Flie*, & the red-legged *Locust*; also, a small *Lacertid*, & a small Yellow *Snake*. Now wth our Fowling Peices, we sett abowte colleckting 1 each of the various Kinds of *Birds*, (indeed, so Tame they was, we scarcely needed our Guns, & had to stand well back from them so as not to damage the Plumage with Shott), a *Buzzard*, a *Short-Eared Owl*, a *Mocking-Thrush*, a yellow *Wren*, a red *Flycatcher*.[2] When we began to examine the *Finches*, we saw they was, tho' so Similar, & all foraging together, of different *Kinds*, at least to Judge by the varying Proportions of theire *Bills*, for some was as Heavy as *Hawfinches*, others slender as a *Wrens*, & with almost every Gradation between. We took what we tho't to be 5 several *Kinds*. We did not take a *Dove*, for we knew the *Boys* had taken severall for Food, & we cou'd skin one of those, & thus not shedd unnecessary Blood.

[2]THESE BE EGSAMPS OF DIFF THEN/TIME BUGS   PICS OF ALL THESE BE RECORD ON MIKE-TAPE   BUG HISTORI BE VERI UP TO DATE WITH NO GAPS

By this Time the *Boys*, most carrying long strings of *Doves* over theire Shou'ders, o'ertook us, & was deleighted wth the *Tortoises*, wch they rode & rac't each other, yipping & hallooing, like the mad *Gachos* of *Patagonia*, (if rather more slowlie!) The *Tortoises* make fine Meat & Oyl, so the *Boys* begin to prepare Slegges to carry some down to the *Boat*.

With the *Boys* sudden Arrival, I had been, as 't were, snappt out of a *Spell* of Absorption; for the Day had scurri'd I knew not whither, in my injoyment of observing these marvelous new Sights, seeing a new System & Interrelation of animate *Nature*: &, I hope, with my Natural-history notes in *Latin*, (much fuller than these my Jottings,) & our colleckting, advanct some small degree the Step by Step Increase in *Mans* Knowledge & understanding; wch one Day, I feel convinct to the bottom of my Soul, will end wth *Man* Knowing & understanding to the last *Iota*, all the interlocking & rational *Systema* of the intire *Cosmos*, wch our most Excellent LORD of all CREATION hath given us for our Deleight & Instruction, as well as our Peace & Confidence in the Ultimate Order & Playne Goodness of all Things. I remarkt the Same to Dr. *Harris*, & even that gruff & skeptickal *Man* agreed.[3]

[This day of glowing confidence in universal order and benevolence is not complete unless I add here the Quartermaster's log entry.]

Sept: 15, off the East-side of *Chatham* Isl. Took aboard: 60 jars of Water; 60 bundles of Faggots; 40 doz. of *Turtle- Dove*; 87 *Tortoise*.

[As you see, my own confidence in the future is not quite so absolute, although as a scientist (amateur grade) myself I can't seem to kick my own interest in finding out more and more.

[3]HOW I WISH I CUD GO BACK SMILING TO TELL THEN/TIME MAN HOW TRU HE SPEAK   HOW ALL HE SAY NOW HAPPEN HOW NOW ALL THINGS BE KNOWED   HOW HIS TRUST IN WE COMES TRU

Maybe in the long run that "absorption" is *it*, the reason, the purpose, and what it leads up to is beside the point. At the moment around here what it is mainly leading up to, all the long slow accretion of knowledge, is two giant nuclear reactors the power company wants to put into operation just nine miles up the virginal river valley from us—just one more indication that there may not even *be* any future. So it begins to seem to me the real question is whether or not we should have a baby.[4]

Dear Abby, We have been married six years, and I am somehow thirty-eight and J is twenty-six. I was already balding when I was seventeen, so I don't suppose I look all that different physically from when I was younger, and we are still, to the neighbors around here, those young kids who watch birds all the time. But I feel myself getting older. Still pretty fit, because we walk so much, usually carrying the tripod and spotting scope, and long-lens camera, the binos, but never to be *really* fit again, too many cumulative things slowly going wrong with the body. So maybe old mortality is a pressure on us. But mainly J is just wasted without a kid.]

It was a new morning.

"Get out of bed, fat fart," J said. She was already standing in front of the window, sun streaming in, taking her nighty off over her head.

"I've spent my whole life looking into windows and never seen

---

[4]HOW WE'S HART GOS OUT TO U MI FREND   IF ONLI I CUD TAKE U 1 DAI SHOW U HOW ALL U'S WORRI/FEAR NOT COMED TO PASS HOW WE'S THINK/TECHS SOLVE ALL PROBS   T H E   U L T I M A T E   S O L V E   EVERYBODI   HAPPI/WARM/FULL   NO   WAR   NO SICK   T E C H S O L V E S A L L   18 CENT 19CENT GUD TIME OF CON-FIDENCE   HAVE TECH HAVE GOD   BUT 20 CENT LEARN THERE BE NO GOD ONLI MAN ONLI TECH   20 CENT MAN LOSED CONFIDENCE   "a crisis of confidence"   NOT BELIEV TECH CAN SOLVE ALL   BUT NO NEEDED TO WORRI/FEAR NOT ONLI NOT BAD TIME NOW BUT VERI MUCH BETTER TIME THEN EVER EVER BEFORE

a thing," he said. "You're the only person I know who never thinks to pull down a shade when you're dressing, and you don't count cause I get to see you anyway."

She wiggled for him. "I notice you're still looking."

"So's the guy in that red car. That's the third time he's come by."

"Oops," she said, backing out of the window. "He did seem to slow down."

She looked back at him smiling, and he thought for a moment she would get back in bed with him. If he said even a word she would, but he felt a sort of tension between them—they hadn't made love since he had started on the book—and he let the moment pass, and she was already putting on her pants.

"What are you going to do today?" she asked.

"Work on the book, then go down to the beach and set up a blind before the tide starts in at noon, and see if I can get some pictures of those Baird's sandpipers. Then I have to go to unemployment this afternoon and pick up a check. What're you going to do?"

"I think I'll start a painting of the western grebe we found on the beach yesterday. Where're you going now?"

"I have to catch some flies for Guinevere and Arthur."

"Anything to put off work."

He took a glass, and a 3 by 5 notecard, out to the east side of the house. Flies were easiest to catch before nine o'clock, collected on the warm sunny wall of the house but still a bit dormant with cold. He put the glass quietly over a large blowfly, then slipped the card between the wall and the mouth of the glass. He brought it in and put it in Guinevere's big gallon coffee jar. She immediately turned her three-cornered head towards the fly, cleaning itself on the opposite side of the jar. She walked over carefully through the foliage, held her heavy grasping arms out in prayer, then darted them forward, seizing the fly and bringing it back to her tiny head, where she began calmly eating the top of the still struggling fly's head.

[13]

"They're getting ready to shed their skins again," J said. "Get a fly for Arthur, and then breakfast will be ready."

He brought in a smaller fly for the male mantis, which was kept in a separate jar, and which was not quite so aggressive, and needed smaller prey. While they ate breakfast they watched him timidly pursuing the fly.

"Probably everything should be fed today," he said. "Is there any fish for Marina?"

"You always start feeding everything, and fixing things around the house, just when you have some work to do. Get cracking on your book."

"You're just the same. You always start spring cleaning the house just when you should be starting a painting."

"Painting is only my hobby. It's my *work* to clean house and have babies."

"Where are the babies?"

"That will have to be up to you, I'm afraid. All our neighbors are impotent alcoholics."

"What chance do I have? You leap out of bed in the morning before I have a chance to grab you."

"That's a lie and you know it. All you have to do is say one word and I'll come back. You're just too old and lazy."

"That's only partly true. Mainly I'm afraid to touch you now that you're doing all this talking about babies."

"Don't you want one?"

"It's completely up to you. You're the one that has to do it all. But it is at least a little bit scary to think about what sort of world he's going to have to live in, everybody chock-a-block in cities, no birds or wildlife left, nuclear reactors giving him leukemia."

"Who says it's going to be a 'him,' sexist pig. And by the way, there's the second public hearing on the reactors tonight. Are you going to go?"

"No, it'll just be a farce."

"You're a terrific citizen."

He took the grebe out of the freezer compartment of the

[14]

refrigerator and put it down on her work table, and also brought out a frozen block of ground beef heart, and scraped some meat off the sides with his pocket knife and dropped the scrapings into an aquarium full of sticklebacks. The fish came up like tiny barracudas, and fiercely tore at the meat. J handed a chicken neck to the one-eyed screech owl waiting on the light fixture over their heads (any injured bird on the island was always brought to them) then followed George out to his study, bringing some smelts for Marina.

The study had originally been the island barber shop, built onto the back of the house by an enterprising former owner. George had his desk in the middle, and bookcases on two sides. The door and windows opened onto the large back yard. The floor was concrete, and for the last four months had been Marina's home. She was a murre, a kind of auk, a foot tall and penguin like. J had found her washed up on the beach, slightly oiled, a long scar down one side, perhaps caused by a boat propeller. At any rate she was afraid to go back into the sea, and probably with reason: the scar separated her feathers, breaking the seal, so probably she would quickly grow waterlogged and freeze or drown in the icy waves. She was very gentle and affectionate, and lived on the floor on a heap of piled up rags and old bedspreads to represent a rock sticking out of water, and had sprayed the lower one-and-a-half shelves of books white with guano. Occasionally, standing behind George while he sat at his desk typing, she would call out to him in a friendly manner—but her call, a long drawn-out waaaaaaaaa meant to be heard through howling winds across a mile of raging sea, turned over the muscles on the back of his neck and made him jump almost to the ceiling.

He sat back down to his work.

* * *

[15]

[Here is the captain again:]
On the 16th Day we pafft thro' good Channels to *Indefatigable*
Ifland, & anchor'd on the N. Side; wth but indiffrent riding, for
the Ground drops away fo fwiftlie, that if the Anchor flipps, it
will not catch agayne; & the Wind perfiftid in coming off the
Land. The Ifland, however, appar'd much more Fertile & Bonnie, well Water'd in Parts, fo at this Place I determin'd to put
Ashoare, a young *Cow* & *Bull*; 3 *Nannies* & a *Billy Gote*; a *Coc-
kerel* & 3 *Henns*, perfuant to my deffeign, to make the more
Hofpitable of the defart Iflands we ftoppt at Fruitfull & Plentifull to *Colonifts*, fo that where now all is houling Wildernefs,
will 1 Day walk *Chriftians* fpredding *Gods* Work. We remayn'd
thro' the 20th, whilft the Boys boyl'd Oyl from the *Tortoifes*; &
from *Seals* & *Guanays* we took in plenty on this Ifland.

[Now Davie, the ship's naturalist (most likely he was a gentleman, a
member of the Royal Society, trained in classics or divinity at Oxford or
Cambridge, largely self-taught in botany, zoology, and geology, his
expenses covered on this voyage, but otherwise unpaid):]

Sept: 16-20. We anchor'd abt. a Quarter of a Mile from Shoar,
Indefatigable Isl. Sea-Birds was now very numberous, *Goneys*,
Pelicums, *Solan Geese*, *Tropick Birds*, *Gulls*, *Mother-Careys Chic-
kens*, *Boatswains Mates*, & others; following Fish Risings, &
feeding in vast noisy Shoals everywhere on the Water. At the
Surface *Sharks* Fins was everywhere to be seen, & gigantic
Mantas broak the Water with theire Wing-Tipps, & regularly
threw theire huge Bulk clear of the Water, & splasht back into it
wth a Report like a Cannonading. From Shoare was the constant
Barking & Roaring from the *Seals*, gather'd in 100's, & the
Stench, from the Land Breaze, nigh unindurable. The grate
Bulls, dubbel & trebbel the Size of theire *Paramoors*, stood up
like proud *Pashas*, daring the next nearest *Bull* even to consider 1
of theire extensive *Harime*, befoare charging & doing bloody
Battle. We fisht from the Decks & brou't in juicy Dorados wth
every Cast, tho' often the *Sharks* & *Barracudies* bit off all but the

Hedd before we cou'd hale em Aboard. There was no casting for larger Fish in deeper Water, for no matter how heavie Weihts we attacht to our Lines, our Lures was taken the moment they toucht Water, nor cou'd we get em even 1 Foot beneath the Surface.

Dr *Harris*, I said, I believe I have cau't you, unawares, quite injoying this Splendid Day, wth ne'er a Grutch nor a Grouse: Here, *Sir*, surely is *Gods* Plentie in its most transparent Aspeck. Nay, he said, smiling at my Plesantrie, but smiling, as his wont, somewhat Wolfishly, too: I have never, in my most Pessimistick Mood, deni'd the singular Bewtie of the *Natural Universe*. There is onelie a verminous *Plague* upon it wch unsettls my Complacencie some what, & that is that scrawnie hareless two-legged *Wretches* who in theire overweening Arrogance believe themselves bro't upon this Marvelous *Erth* to Rule it, & theire Notion of "Rule" is the very same Notion as your *Pirates* who preceeded us to these Islands, wch is to Rape & Pillage & turn all to theire contempnable Idea of "Profitt". I carry an *Image* in my Brayne wch makes me shudder; of a *World* ultimately divested of all *Life* but this dispickable 1 of our own *Kind*. Look wth your smiling Eys shoarward a Moment, where our *Fellows* have lately debark'd. You can see em from here, strippt Nakid to save theire Cloaths from Gore, like Revolting *Monkies* wth outsiz'd Genitals as they step thro' the Crouds of *Seals*, smashing an Innocent & incomprehending *Cranium* wth each Swing of theire Clubbs.[5] Ah

[5]MI GUD FRIEND DR   THER IS MUCH (WTH UR GUD HART) U DO NOT SEE   MAN IS GUD   LOOK FOR EGSAMP AT URSELF   LOOK AT DAVIE   GUD PEOPLE   NOW LOOK "shoarward" AT UR "*Fellows*" & U SEE TERRIBUL/HORRIBUL "killing" & BLOOD   BUT WHY? ASK URSELF

BECUZ IN WORLD THERE BE "*Sharks*" WCH "kill" "*Fish*" WCH "kill"   ECT   WHAT UR/TIME CALL "dog eat dog"

WHEN MAN LIVED IN SUCH-LIKE A WORLD   HAD TO DO LIKEWISE   WORLD "red in tooth and claw"   NOW NO MORE   HOW MUCH U WUD LIKE WE'S NOW/WORLD AFTER T H E   U L T I M A T E S O L V E NO MORE "fight"   NO MORE "kill"   (NO MORE EVEN HAVE THESE WORDS IN NOW/LANG)   ONLI PEACE   ONLI LOVE

[17]

but! I replied: look abowte you at the *Birds* diving for *Fish*, the *Sharks* gulping down what they can get within theire *Maws*, the Water virtually seething wth *Fish* eating *Fish*. This, *Sir*, is the Fact upon wch *Life* is founded, & *Man* no more Singular in this than any other *Creatur* wch must eat to Live. Surely we have argu'd this often enough, that 't is all of a *System*; in wch each takes, & ultimately gives, so that in the long Run an *Equality* prevayles. All but in the Case of our own debas'd *Kind*, *Sir*, he repli'd bitterlie. He takes, & takes, & takes. & what does he ever *give*? You saw yourself, when we was Ashoare Yesterday, he had left behind him onelie his stincking Pat of Shite behind every Bowlder & Bush, & when he dies finally, onelie his reeking *Corse*, too fowell for any but the *Maggots* to batten on. Ah but, ah but! said I, in *Triumph*, Do not these very *Maggots*, fat sleak & nourisht by our healthful *Corses*, provide Provender for the *Birds* of the Field, who feed the *Fox*, who is eat by the *Lion*, who is swallo'd, drinking incautiously from the Sea, by the *Shark*, who is stunn'd by the Fluke of the *Whale*, & washes ashoare & fertilizes, wth his *Carcass*, the Desart, out of wch grows the Grasses that feed the *Hind* who supplies the pot of once agayne *Man*, compleating the *Circle*!

Dr *Harris*, cou'd not contayne himself from laughing merrily at this my *Invention*, but he did not miss the poynt of it niether. Perhaps, perhaps, *Davey*, I hope it is just as you say: For if I was once finally convinc't that all of *Man Kind* was as fowell, as Deprav'd, as Valewless to the general *Oeconomie*, as I am myself in my inmost *Hart*, I wou'd in Despair this instant hurl myself into the gnashing *Fangs* of your helpfull & benevolent *Sharks*; as indeed, in more gradual Fashion, I suppose I was doing, in leaving my *London* Pracktise & coming this *John* o' *Bedlem* Journey. But *Davey*, you don't know how much your own undoubted Goodness, & your often very well Reason'd Optimism, have given me Pause.

[Dr. Harris's papers are the most difficult to deal with. He wrote out of that itch to write which seems to have infected the whole of the 18th century in western Europe, but also, pretty clearly, out of a strong need to examine as objectively and rationally as he could manage his own thoughts and actions; he wrote, in short, for therapy. He certainly didn't write for posterity, as is evidenced by his extremely crabbed and difficult hand, and by the fact that he neither dated nor paginated nor so much as mentioned a place name to help his harried editor place his papers relative to the others. Also, I suspect he was a wealthy or at least a comfort-loving man, for he wrote on a very fine, soft, heavy paper, which our old sourdough may have favored for his personal use. Anyway, the Dr.'s papers were the most scattered and fragmented. This next entry, however, pretty obviously locates itself here by internal evidence.]

The slougter of the Innocents was well advanct, when *Davey*, & I, & the beeming Cpt. went Ashoare for the 2d Time. *I have a Pisgah Vision, Gentlemen*, quothe the good Cpt, *whr now all is houling Wilderness, will 1 Dai walk Christains spredding Gods Word*. We landed on a 2d small Beech, well awaye from that of the *Seels*, wch was now running heavy & stagnant wt Gore almost out to the *Shipp*, in order to save our Shoos & Stockins. We cou'd heer at 1 End of the *Rookerie*, wch the *Boys* had n't reecht yet, the bellowing of the *Bulls* challenging thr *Rivals*, the Barking of the *Cows*, the Bleeting of the *Calves*, continu'ing Eatch in his usual Waye, all unwares of the Death Screams of woundid & maimd slouly working its implacable Waye tourds em. *Davey*, & I, stood back whilst Mr *Mountague*, & Little *Jemmie*, pulld off a Brace of *Cattle*, the *Gotes*, the *Fowell*, & drove em, clapping thr Handes, up the 1st brittle Incline. Stony *Iguanas* sat atop the Mounds of thr *Bourrows*, blincking Stupidly at the new *Colonists*. The *Gotes* at once begun eating doun to the *Root* the scatter'd Bits of *Herbage*. The *Cow* was Ripe, & the *Bull* followed her Step by Step, Nose up her *Vulva*. The Cpt walkt back to us, brushing his Handes & puffing. *I see solid Howses spring up*, he said, *the fertile upper Slopes plantid to Mayze or some such Tropickal Fruits, & a thriving Industrie of Seel & Whale Oyl, ('t Is True, the Anchorage cd be finer,) but 1 Dai Christain white Man, will inhabit the intirety of this Orbis Terrarum, as the Lord God intendid it from the Beginning. & we shall have plai'd our small Part, Gentlemen.*[6]

I might have spoke to this Pt; but I am a Cowardly Nature. & besides, how can one place a Shaft of Dou't into so Innocent & Trusting & Unquestioning a *Hart?* I might have satisfi'd myself to share a Look wt *Davey*, whoo knowes my thou'ts, whether he shares em; but that good *Man* had wanderd off from us to observe 2 *Iguanas* attempning to couple wt the same Feemale. *Exactly as the little Sand Lizzards at Home*, he shouted back in deleight!

Little *Jemmie*, as prettie & soft a *Lad* as ever shippt Cabins *Boy*, a grate favourite of us all, wt some thing fyne in his feeturs suggesting he was Heir to a better Fortune then he has had, strippt off his *Vest* & *Trowsers*, & dove into the Surf, & immergd beyond, his smooth broun *Arms* & *Shou'ders* out of the Water as he swam stronglie, & dove, & sportid, like a very *Seel* himself. A feer crosst mee: *What of Sharks*, I said to Mr *Montague? You 'ware of Sharks, my Deer*, the Cpt calld to him. *Arr! Sir, they shawnt bovver wi li'l mee, wi so much Seel Guts just 1 Mile doun the Beech.* He prudentlie came in, however, & stretcht out on the Sand on his *Back* just beelow wher we was sitting.

Shall wee find some Spot Inland to have our Tay & Bisketts, the Cpt. said? Nay, if ye dont mind, I said, this Spot likes me here, wt a *See* Vuw.

Sept: 20, *Indefatigable* Isl. Took aboard: 41 Barrels *Seal* Oyl; 3 cwt dry'd *Fish*; 50 doz. of *Turtle- Dove*; 45 bundles of Faggots.

* * *

[6]"Orbis Terrarum" = ALL QUADS   THIS TO MUCH TRU MI GUD CAP   NOW WE HABIT ALL QUADS   NO MORE "houling Wilderness" TO BE UGLI TO TAKE FOOD FRUM WE'S MOUTH TO MAKE WE SICK NOW ONLY TO MUCH HAPPI WE OVER ALL AN YES U EXPLOR/MAN PLAYDED U "small Part"!

It was a week later.

"You *are* comical," J said, "eating your potato soup and fahting."

"Eating my potato soup and 'fotting'?"

"Eating your po*tah*to soup and fahting, you lame American mother fucker."

They were having a lazy day. He had pottered around all morning reading Bannerman's *Birds of the British Isles*, the volume on waders, which J's folks had been sending him, volume by volume, as a sort of on-going birthday/Christmas present. Now it was lunchtime, J still wasn't dressed, standing at the sink in her sleek silky 1930's pink nighty, down to the floor, but emphasizing every line of her butt, which was towards him. It was a cool fall morning. George sort of liked roughing it, but J had insisted on putting on the furnace for the first time, and it had filled the house with the smell of burning dust, a smell he liked, reminding him of foggy summer mornings in Berkeley, where he grew up, when you would wake up with the furnace ticking and crackling with expansion, a week or two's accumulation of dust burning off its surface. The house was now, he had to admit, very pleasantly warm. J came over behind his chair, and put her arms around his neck, and kissed the back of his head. He held himself a bit stiffly. There was a tension, they both felt it now. They had not made love for a full week. Their sex always went in cycles, hot and heavy and constant for a few days, then they got out of it for several days, and he started building up a tension, thinking about it more and more, but as if there was a block between them and he hesitated to touch her, and it didn't seem like he could kiss her properly, or make her respond, and he felt like an oaf pawing her, and he would leave her alone, except he kept seeing her and thinking about her. Even after six years a night had not passed that he hadn't watched her get undressed.

Which she did, by the way, as undramatically, as untheatrically as possible. No matter what she was wearing, with no notion of suspense she always took off her panties first, either stepping out of them if she was wearing a dress, or grabbing panties and the top of her trousers with the same grip, and pushing down both together. She never had the least shyness with any part of her body, even her bum, which he himself was rather shy with. Before she came over so they could get married, he used to have little obscene fantasies where he would imagine they were already married, living in some hot humid climate, and he would say, gosh, you would certainly be more comfortable doing your ironing or whatever if you took off your clothes, at least to your panties and bra, to do it, but in fact when they did get married, it seemed like she was almost constantly naked around the house, there was almost nothing she did throughout the day that didn't involve her taking off her clothes, and always so casual about it. He decided that was a European thing. American girls were always either shy about their bodies, or made a big production out of it, or coquetted with it, but Europeans (within his limited experience) were absolutely matter-of-fact. That went for touch, too. With American girls you had to follow the sort of rigid strip-tease order, tits, then you work up to (or down to) thighs, then last cunt, each step a milestone in your relationship, at first resisted, then grudgingly given in to. But with European girls it seemed like it was either all there for you from the start, or it was not. If you could touch any part, they let you touch every part, an absolute equality of parts, with no taboo zones (except for French girls, that you can do anything at all to, except you can't kiss them on the lips, because that's reserved for True Love).

"Are you going to the third nuclear reactor hearing tonight?" She was back at the sink.

"Oh, is that tonight? Shit. I don't feel much like going out. We'll go to the next one."

"We should go to at least one of them."

"Why? Do you think we should be worrying about 'its' future?"

"I don't know where 'it's' going to come from if you don't get to work."

[22]

"*Me?* Every time I touch you, you start snoring."

"You never let that stop you before."

"That's cause I never noticed the difference."

"Oh *boy*, listen to him. You're so bloody insensitive something as good as me is totally wasted on you."

"I'm going to take a bath," he said.

"That will improve the air in here a great deal."

"What needs improving in this house is that big pile of snot standing by the sink." He ran up behind her—her hands were full of dishes, so she was defenseless—and started tickling her sides, and she started shrieking. Then he lifted up her nighty and pressed up against her bum, and suddenly, click, all the tension was gone, all the reserve, and she was reaching around undoing his belt, and they were gasping, and rubbing against each other, and he pushed her over on the counter and went into her from behind.

He was reading in bed when she finally came to bed for the night. She crawled over him and lay down with her face to the wall. He snuggled up behind her, crotch to bum, arms around her breasts, which was how they always went to sleep, but he could feel her shaking and shaking, which either meant she was laughing hilariously, or sobbing, he could never tell which, until finally he reached up to her face and felt the tears. He waited patiently, and at last she told him.

"I'm such a coward," she said. "It's the start of a new cycle, and I took my pill. Oh *hell*."

* * *

[Here's a section in the Dr.'s hand which I can't satisfactorily work in anywhere. Sometime after they were at the Galapagos, they were in the South Seas as well. This entry, obviously, is from that period.]

We was some 500 Leagues W of the *Mayne*, when we spy'd the *Island*, alreddy almost to farr to the S for us to pick up in the suddenlie Contrarie Winds. We spent 4 Dais beeting doun to it. It seemd to us fixt in 1 Spott, & we fixt in another, but almost inperceptiblie it grew higher & higher, standing strai't out of the See, cappt by giant Thunder Hedds, lush thick *Forrest* beelow, & as we came up on it, we saw the long line of *Surf* braking over the proteckting outer *Reefs*, & *Co-Co Palms* lining the white inner *Strand*.

'Is like a Vision of *Paradise* unfolding, *Davey* said; & when I turnd to him in a Moment, I saw large round *Teers* falling from his *Eys*. What is it so moves thee in the thou't of *Paradise, Man?* & then: Mayhap I know; is it the thou't of whoo awaits thee there? *Debra* was onelie 17. he said. We marri'd of Love, wch is why Im a poor *Man* to this Dai, for my *Father* had rich Prospecks pickt out for me. The very 1st *Babe* got bound up in her somehow, & was onelie borne after 3 hellish Dais, & I said, hoping to cheer her, *Debra, 't is a bonnie Girl*, & she said: *Lord God that means 1 Day she must suffer as I am suffring Now*. What does a *Man* answer to that, *George?* I said in my *Hart*, if she survive, I shall never toutch her agayne; but in the next 8 Dais I watcht her wilt awaye, & droop, & dye; & for several *Months* I car'd not how soon I jin'd her. When I heerd of this *Voyage*, I jumpt at it, hoping the Change wou'd mend me, & it has, a Bit; for tho' I know I have myself been cast out from *Lifes* Feest, I see now cleerlie that the Feest itself continu's, & this gives me a sad sort of Twilight Pleasur in the Beholding it, tho' I be forever cut off from the Partaking.

I might have said, 't is a *Cannibal* Feest thou'rt well quit of: Instedd: Thou'rt Young yett, *Davey*; thou'lt marry agayne & have many sunny *Babes*. For Answer: he but toucht my *Arm*, & sadly shook his *Hedd*.

Mr *Mountague*, jin'd us at the *Bow*, We was just remarcking, *Sir*, the Bountifull & pleasing Aspeck of the *Land*. Hm, said he, smoothing his beerd, but I notice in 4 Dais we have seen neither

Boat nor Spume of Smoak nor other sign of *Life*. Most like there is no waye into the *Reef*.

Abt Noon of the 4th Dai we hove to abt 1 Mile from the *Reefs*, & sent the *Pinace* out to explor for an opning. It struck 1 at once, & ledd us into a safe Deep *Harbour*, where we anchord befor Dark, but not knowing if ther bee salvage *Natives* or salvage *Beests* ashoare, we prudentlie held off landing till the following Dai. At 1st Light we was dumbfoundid to see that the *Beech*, wch had been emptie, now had grate Piles of *Goods* upon it. Throu' the Perspecktive *Glass* we cou'd see that *Co-Co Nuts, Fruits,* & several new slougter'd *Hoggs* lay upon the *Beech*, apparentlie waiting our Pleasur, but still no Sign of *Habitants*.

't Is a Peece Offring, said *One*.

't Is an Ambuscade, said *Tother*.

If they want Peece, they surely shall have it, said Mr *Montague*, & we shall take Ashoar a *Chest* of the *Knives* little *Ax*'s, & *Mirrours* wch we brou't for *Gifts*. However if they have trecherie in Mind, we shall also come wt a Partie of *Muskets*, but let me be Cleer; ther shall be no fireing or shewing of *Armes* intill you have my express Word, & that Word shall come onelie if we are in Grave & immediate Daunger. We took the 2 *Longboats* & went Ashoar in a Partie 30 Strong, & left 30 beehind to gard the *Shipp*. Here we found 20 fine *Hoggs* fresh killd & wrappt in *Palm* leaves, grate Mounds of *Co-Cos* & *Plantaynes*, & other very fine *Fruits* wch we sampld & found very Savourie.

Then the *Boys* commenct Hooping & Wisling, then 1, then 4, then 4 & 20 Native *Woemmen*, stark Nakid, emergd from the *Forrest* Edg smiling & laughing & thro'ing up thr *Armes* in Greeting. 'Ware of Trecherie, my *Boys*, the Cpt said, but was heeded onelie a Moment, for ther was no mistaking the intention of the Dusky *Vahines*, giggling & rolling on the Ground & obscenlie exposing thr *Partes* beefore the Gloating *Men*, who befor all our *Eys* was soon coupling[7] wt em like so many *Cattel*, guffawing back to ther *Comrads* at this unexpecktid *Boon*. I remonstratid wt Mr. *Montague*, but that sober Religious *Man* said Nay, I know 't is unseemlie, but Im convinct the *Lord* has suppli'd us these Dark *Races* to give the *Boys* a chaunce to Relieve themselves, & emptie themselves out. I think ther can be no Harm in 't, for I have seen it often to bee on past *Voyages*, that we shall see less fighting & bickring Aboard. As a Chirurgian ye must know, 't is a necessitie to Health—& as I continu'd to look at him: Come, *Man*, we are all humane *Beeings* together. 't Is not like they are Christain *Woemmen*, & he lookt upon me so impatiently for me to betake myself elswhere, that I at last realiz'd my judging *Eys* was preventing his own disporting; so I rather sharplie took *Davey* by the *Arme*, Let us explor Inland a Wayes, said I.

We passt thro' the thin line of *Palms* back of the *Beech*, but cou'd ascertayne no Trayles into the Interior, or Sign any where of humane *Habitation*, but yet the *Countrie* was open, softlie rounded & smiling, wt none of the harsh Grittiness some times on Tropick *Isles*, & all growing things O'er burdnd wt *Fruit*, *Co-Co Nuts*, *Bananos*, *Pawpaws*, *Mango's*, the going Easy, along the mossy Bank of a slender pure *Spring*, meandring thro' a deep *Valley*, whilst the denser *Forrest* crawld up the steep Slopes to Mountayn Tops lost in the Cascading white Mists above us.

I think you was quite right *Davey*, if *Paradise* exist, it must bee in terms very like these. He had stoppt & turnd, for 3 of the Native *Girls* was running wt all thr Might to catch us up. Ignore em, I said, there as Forward as *Convent Garden* Fireships, & carry *Lord* kno's what Jungle Blights & Cankers. But they cleverlie chang'd ther Stratigy, (once they puffingly reacht us,) & as it were, cover'd themselves over wt Blushes & Bashfullness, especially a very young plump *Thing*, barely Sproutid, who hid

---

7"couple" = FUK THERE SEEM TO BE MUCH EVIDENS THAT THEN/ TIME MAN DID TRULI FUK WITH ANIMALS BUT CUD NOT OF CORSE HAVE CHILDS DURING THEN/TIME MANI QUADS HAVE ONLI ANI-MALS (THIS BEFOR DEVELOP) SOME AFRICAN (BLACK) AN CHINA (YELLO) ANIMALS STILL CAN BE SEED IN ANIMAL PARK IN NW ATLAN-TIC QUAD ALL ANIMALS RECORD ON MIKE-TAPE THIS KIND HERE CAN BE SEED UNDER "Polynesian"

behind the others, & cover'd her *Eys*, & peept out at *Davey*. This shyness is the oldest, most pracktist Trick of all, *Davey*, think on "The Bowre of Bliss", but *Davey* was smittn, & no dou't. She lay on the Mossy Bank befor him, & every seeming attemp to conceal her Nakidness to him onelie expos'd it the more. Dost speak any *Christian* Tongue,[8] *Davey* said? Hablas Espagnole? but she spoke onelie a more Universal Tongue, beckning him & moving modestlie off into the *Bushes*. He lookt at mee in the gratist extremitie of Confusion, then rusht off following her.

Her 2 coarser *Companions* now clos'd wt mee, grinning & pulling at my cloathing, & touchting mee. Hands off the Propertie my *Deers*, I said, & made cleer to em ther stayle *Flesh* mov'd me no more than a *Monkies*, & then 1 of the forward Hussy's undid my *Trowser* tops & begin to pull em down, whilst tother pulld open the Bottons on my *Blowse*; & ther *Hands* was so Nimble, & they ract' abowte mee wt such Speed, wch I cou'd scarse follow, my cloathing abowte my *Knees*, that struggle how I wou'd, short of striking em, or showing Violence,—tho' I lookt it in my *Eys*, & thretnd it verbally, in very few Moments I found myself quite stript of Cloaths, & now was hartily glad *Davey* had deboucht wt his *Paramour*, so I was spar'd having him witness my ludicrouse Predickament.

Well they cou'd now see quite visiblie ther blandishments had no Power to move mee, & had a quick Council of War & then laught till Teers came to ther *Eys*: & 1 rusht off, whilst tother mov'd off more slowlie, beckning mee to follow, & to be certayne I wou'd, carri'd off my Cloaths wt her.

They carri'd mee up a side *Valley*, mossy & *Tree* dappld, & then my *Escort* quite disappeard, & I was left on my own, & thou't this was perhaps some Prank they play'd mee, to show ther disgust for mee, but beefore I had a chaunce to throw on my

---

[8]THEN/TIME MAN BELIEVED ANIMALS CAN SPEAK   WE KNO NOW THIS WAS ONLI MIMIC SOUND   ALL ANIMAL SOUNDS BE RECORD ON MIKE-TAPE WITH NO GAPS

Cloaths, I found that this was not ther Desseign at all.

A Yong *Boy* appar'd, round & plump as the *Girl* who had seduc't *Davey*. Unlike the wanton *Woemmen* he wore a bit of bark Clout abt his *Loynes* to Proteck,—tho' but imperfeckly—his Modestie. He brou't mee a fresh *Co-Co Nut*, & puncturd it quicklie wt his little Knife, & gave mee to drink the refreshing Draught of wholsom Water within, & when I had finisht, he expertlie split it in a Moment, & gave mee to eat of the juicey *Flesh*, as savourie as any thing I remember eating, & gazing upon mee the whole *Time* wt his wide sober *Eys*, at once smiling if he cau't mee looking back at him. Straunge as it seems, I had not once recall'd I was quite Nakid, but all at once I did, & no dou't flusht wt Embarrassment; wch wt grate Sensitivitie he seem'd to realize, tho' in this backwards *Land* I am certayne such nicities as covering ones *Partes* but seldom occur'd to em, but now wt the most exquisite Tackt, he divestid himself of his own little Breeches Clout to put us, as 't were, upon an Equalitie, & he invited mee to come into the stream & bathe wt him, where it was partially dammd & backt up into a little *Pond*. The Water was most wonderfullie Cool, & he disportid abowt like a *Frogg*, kicking & diving, wch was very pretty to beehold, & sometimes boldlie coming & wresling mee into it, but in the gentlist fashion, & he brou't a fine white *Sand* from the Bank & using it like a *Sope* he washt my *Back* & *Sides* & *Leggs*, & then, tho' he demurr'd shylie at 1st, he let me wash him as well, & the more I toucht him the more he smil'd; intill there wou'd be no mistaking that we both knew full well what we was abowte.

[There is a very interesting postscript to this idyllic interlude, still in the Dr.'s hand, which would certainly have been lost, except that the Dr. deliberately attached it to the backside of the sheets on which the foregoing account is written.

I must confess that when I was reading of the account of their visit to this island, it never occurred to me that there was a very strange, even sinister undertone to everything that happened. A smiling island full of food, with safe harborage, and yet no sign of human habitation. Yet when they stop before it, they are presented with a large mysterious gift of food, and are greeted by a handful of more than friendly natives. On the surface, it is every young man's dream of a tropical isle. But when you stop to think about it: no houses, no other people except the welcoming committee—

Here is the explanation:]

Lett mee annex this here, for my Account of this *Isle* is not done. after a Morning of Franck Carousing, the *Men*,—Fair play to the Cpt—pulld to wth a spirit, & wee loadid the *Shipp* wt abundance of Food & Water & Fire Wood. However, in the Evening when wee returnd to the *Shipp*, 3 *Men* was missing. Wee holloo'd them for an Howre, but no response. At 1st wee feerd Trecherie, but then some of the *Boys* confesst they had heerd them say they plannd to jump *Shipp* here, determind, it wou'd seem, to injoy these willing *Woemmen* for a *Life* Time.

The next intire Daye wee searcht the *Island*, loath to lose 3 good *Hands*. Wee had alreddie lost 25 Men from sickness & Accident, & cou'd ill afford to lose more, wt more then half our *Journey* still befor. But wee found ne'er a Trace of the *Men*, &,—strange to relate,—ne'er a Sign of the *Woemen*, or indeed of *any* Humayne *Life*, niether *Dwelling*, nor *Cattel*, nor *Canoa*, & wonderd if wee had dreamt the preceeding Dai. Much bemus'd, & sorely vex'd, wee Sayld off.

Four Monthes later, when we was hedding E once more, on our return to the *Mayne*, wee came back bye, & stoppt agayne. The cpt was confident that by then the 3 wou'd have had enough of *Musketos* & raw *Fish* & salvage Conversation, & wou'd humbly begg leave to rejine us, wch, after pretending grate severity, he wou'd allow them.

Indeed, when wee was still a full Dayes journey from the *Isle*, but cloas enough that wee wou'd be in Vuw to someone on it, wee at once saw a grate Bon Fire lighted to beckon us, & when wee anchord, & took the *Men* off the *Isle*, they provd to bee the wretchidess most miserable beeings imaginable, & fell weeping at the Cpt's Feet, begging his forgiveness. So obviously Penitent was they, that hee quickly gave em full Pardon; & now there Teers of Joy was equal to those, formerly, of ther Distress.

Ther Story, when at length wee got it from em, was sufficientlie Horrid: The 3, once they had determind to jump *Shipp*, went deep into the *Forrest* with 3 of the *Woemmen*. When the *Woemen* realized what they was abowte, in the most frantick manner they gestur'd for em to return, & was quite beside themselves, when at length wee gave over hallooing them & returnd to the *Shipp* that 1st Night. They thou't wee wou'd leave then, & after a long debayte, the *Woemmen* took Pitty on em, & ledd em a long Waye in Land; but in a very curious Waye, walking far apart from each other, so as not to make a *Trayle*, & wt Twiggs brushing out ther Foot Stepps beehind them. At length they took them to apparantlie an emptie Landskip, & carefullie uncover'd the Mowthe to a *Cave* so ingeniusly conceal'd, the sharpist *Ey* cou'd ne'er have detecktid it, & in a twinckling 2 of the *Woemmen* had vanisht doun it; the 3d gesturing wt Frantick impatience for the *Saylors* to follow, so shee cou'd quicklie conceal the Intrance agayne. Wt grate trepidation, at length they interd, a Narrow Waye they must crawl in *Hedd* 1st on there *Bellies*, scarce Room enough around them to Move, & at once they was plungd in intense *Darkness*.

Beeing Wild & scapegrace foolhardly Tarpaulins, [ed. hence, our expression "tars" for sailors] they made the best Face on it, & squirmd forward, dropping doun a steep Slope for a considerable distance, wt all the Terrours of beeing swallow'd Alive in the *Erth*, but cheering 1 tother on, & at Length detecktid Light ahead, & came out into a very large *Room*, hott, smokey, & litt by Torches. As they stood up to stretch ther Bones, they was suddenly layd hold of by a dozayne brauny *Salvages*, who at once overpowerd em, & bound em tightly wt Ropes. 't Was in this miserable *State* they passt the following Dai, when wee was sertching for em, & wou'd, had wee known it, but too happily have answer'd our Calls. For the next severall Dais, onelie there *Arms* bound now, they was taken thro' an extensive Series of underground *Caverns*, & here was the *Islands* Population, 100s of

Men, Woemmen, & *Children, Dogs, Cattel, Piggs,* living despritly under the *Erth,* & obviously on a full War footing, the *Men* constantly heavily Armd wt wood Swords, heavy Clubbs, & Speers, going out in small Scouting Parties by Dai, whilst the rest cowerd underground, never eating more than tiny Bitts of Food at a Time, so they wou'd alwayes bee ready to fight there hardist, never relaxing, or sleeping more then a few *Howres* at a stretch.

All this Time, our *Boys* cou'd see they was debayting what to do wt em; & expecktid to be slougterd at any Moment; & when at ⌐ength the *Indians* seemd to have come to a decision abowte them; & unbound them, (but brandishing severall Speers at em,) & forc'd them to craul once more to the Surface, but by a diffrent Waye, coming up on a Part of the *Island* they hadnt seen beefor, they thou't ther *Time* had come, & teerfully said Good Bye to 1 tother. But, after leeding em a confusing Waye doun to the *Beech,* the *Indians* meerly meltid into the *Forrest* & they realiz'd they had been sett Free. They even found, left neer em, there little bundle of *Bisketts* & *Rum* they had brou't with em, (but had left at the 1st Cave *Mowthe,* when they had 1st interd the Caves wt the *Woemmen,*), &, best of all, the *Salvages* had also left them ther *Muskets* & *Pouder,* not kno'ing what ther Use was.

Now they made shift as best they cou'd, on an *Island* wich seemd devoyde of *Life,* thou' they knew a whole *Nation* liv'd in *Caves* beneeth em. They made themselvs a *Shelter,* cou't *Fish,* huntid *Piggs,* ate *Fruit,* & constantlie had 1 *Man* on watch in case our *Shipp* sou'd return, & sett up an immense Bon Fire on the *Beech* to Signal wt. But alwayes too in the back of there *Hedds,* was the feer that whoever the *Islanders* livd in such Terrour of wou'd come Bye.

At length 1 Dai the *Man* watching on the *Beech* came running up the Mountayne to locate his *Fellows* wt the Terrifying News that the whole *Baye* had filld wt *Canoas.* They lookt doun from a *Hedd Land* & saw the *Beech* swarming wt Dark Nakid *Salvages,* heavily armd, bones in there *Noses, Teeth* fild to poynts. They now heerd grate shouting & laughing, & suddaynely saw the self-same Greeting Partie of Nakid *Vahines,* & soon a very *Dyony-*

[31]

sian Scene was beefor. But then there was a Shout, & they had discover'd the *Saylors* Shelter. Now there was grate excitement & shouting. The *Salvages* quicklie pickt up there Trayle, & came rushing up the *Hedd Land*. The *Men* chargd there *Muskets*, & bravely put themselves in Battle Line, determind to sell there lives deerly. They agreed that 2 wou'd Fire, & leave the 3d Gun in reserve whilst they was re-charging. The *Salvages*, having no *Idea* what a *Musket* was, strode right up to them, either to dash out ther *Braynes*, or take them Prisoner. When they was but 15 ft distant, the *Boys* opend up, mortally wounding 5 of em wt there 1st *Volley*. But 't was probably the Explosion, the Flash, the puff of black *Pouder* that had the most effeck, for the *Salvages* turnd pell mell & boltid for there *Shipps* & within 15 *Minutes* the last *Canoa* had paddld out of the *Harbour*.

The *Boys* expectid now to bee treetid like *Heros* for saving the *Island* from *Cannibals*, but in fackt the *Woemmen* had vanisht at the 1st *Alarm*; & they had perforce to spend another miserablie loneli 2 *Months* waiting our return, constantlie in Feer of a new Attack, whilst the bodies of there slayne *Enemies* Bloted & Stank & Liquifi'd in the hott *Sun*.

Davey did not miss his chaunce to Twitt mee: Ah! said hee, if onelie wee cou'd return to that life of *Peece & Tranquillitie* of our *Primal Parents*! Modern *Man* has not inventid *War*, I own'd to him,—onelie: he has improv'd 100 fold the *Ingines* of Destrucktion. Where is the difference to the *Victim*, said hee, betwixt having his *Braynes* disht out by a Clubb, or beeing bloun apart in a Cannonading? Then, said I, you confess there has been no *Progress*? The *Progress*, said hee, is in *Moral* Institutions wich will 1 Dai have the Ascendencie over *Mans* primitive *Nature*, & then indeed our Ingines shall be beet into *Plough Shares* of Universal Benefiscense. If they dont blow us off the *Erth* betimes, quoth I. *Grutch Grutch*, said hee, laughing, & pouring mee more Tay.[9]

[9]DAVI SPEAK TO MUCH TRU   NOW WE'S "Moral Institutions" OVER ALL   NO MORE "primitive Nature" ANIMALS TO START WAR   ONLI TO MUCH HAPPI WE

[I said at the beginning that I intended, from time to time, to add certain writings of my own to this volume, when they seemed apposite. This is an essay I wrote for the local Audubon Society *Newsletter* (which I happen to be editor of—one useful perogative of being editor is everything you submit is automatically accepted), and which got a nice response, and which is now going to be reprinted in the new journal, *Environmental Essays*.]

A STILLAGWUMP ISLAND CALENDAR

by George Herbert

We live on Stillagwump Island (a peninsula, actually) in a small house set back from the road, with few other houses about, trees and fields on three sides, and down at the end of the front lawn, a steep, hundred-foot drop to the beach below, and the long, shallow mudflats of Smiley Bay stretching south to Waterville.

It was in the fall of the year that we first moved in, a still, cloudless Indian Summer. To the east of us, the snow cap of Mt. Baker glowed in the afternoon sun, blushed orange in the evening, faded to purple. A hundred or so miles to the south, a phantom-like Mt. Rainier rose above the Seattle smog. Of course we were interested in nature, or we would not have decided to live so far from my teaching job in Mt. Pleasant, but our interest was general, and perhaps rather casual. Stillagwump Island seemed to be filled with birds, so, for the moment, we thought we would try to learn something about birds.

The first thing we saw was that a swallow had nested that summer on our front porch, had plastered his half-circle of mud up under the supports of the porch roof, and left an impressive pile of dirty-white guano on the cement floor beneath. The nest was at eye level, and we hoped he would use it again next year, so we could watch the whole family-raising process through the living-room window. But for now, all the swallows had long since finished their nesting for the year, and the whole neighborhood was teeming with them, all gathered here on the edge of the water, fattening up on swarms of midges, before migration. We got out our Peterson *Guide to the Western Birds* and tried to pick through the various species. The handsome tropical looking ones with the pinkish-buff breasts and long trailing, deeply forked "swallow" tails, were of course barn swallows. It was one of these who had made the nest on the porch. Those with the buff-colored rump and the intricate, richly-colored facial patterns were cliff swallows, birds we had seen before, nesting under bridges in the mid-west. There were new species as well. Birds with white underparts and plain blue-black backs were tree swallows; almost identical birds, but with a flash of white coming up on each side around the base of the tail, were violet-green swallows. When these last turned into the sun, their backs were shot with green, and below the white rump, the tops of their tails flashed violet.

This was a good start, to see all these species about the house, and in such vast numbers (in late afternoon, the telephone wires solid lines of these trim little birds, sitting shoulder to shoulder in hundreds or perhaps thousands). In the evenings Brewer's and red-winged blackbirds and starlings gathered in noisy flocks, flying round and round the neighborhood in perfect formation, settling in first this tall tree, then that, before, as it began growing dark, they all drifted off at last to a thick stand of firs out back, where they roosted for the night. Last thing in the evening, the sky green and gold at the horizon, we would hear the nasal *peent peent* of the nighthawks, coursing invisibly through the high night sky, their calls falling like the disembodied spirits of the dying summer.

A good start. But having identified these birds, and watched them with appreciation, we might have gone on to something else, except one day, just at the beginning of October, most of the swallows gone by now, I glanced out the front window and saw an immense black bird just plummeting out of my line of sight below the cliff. I shouted to my wife, and she came running, bringing with her the battered, twenty-year-old pair of six-power binoculars we shared between us. In a moment the bird reappeared, flapping heavily, carrying a small glistening white seagull in its talons, and landed on the snag top of the tallest fir tree down at the end of our front yard. It was an immature bald eagle. Trading the binoculars back and forth, we watched him rip the hapless gull apart, and devour him, while a snow of white feathers drifted tranquilly down and slowly covered our lawn.

An eagle in our own front yard! We were hooked. I bought a second pair of binoculars with my first check, and a book on Washington Birds. I built a bird feeding tray and propped it on a pole just a few inches outside the kitchen window, and covered the tray and the surrounding driveway with birdseed.

By this time, of course, we had followed the narrow trail down the cliff to the beach, and seen in the water a hundred feet offshore some two dozen loons swimming along together, barking, hooting, and laughing maniacally. Lovely enormous birds, the size of geese, or larger, a black collar about the white neck, a pattern of round white circles on the greenish black back, long heavy black bills, lean submarine outline—at a signal they would all dive, and suddenly the crowded bay was empty. Precisely these same wonderful big primitive birds (why evolve, when you are already perfect?) were swimming the seas a hundred million years ago, when water covered the center of what is now the United States, and swam alongside the fabulous *Hespornis*, a giant flightless seabird extinct long before man was ever thought of, and dove down to where six-foot-long marine scorpions scuttled across the sea-bottom ooze of Iowa and Illinois.

After a few humiliating days when our bird-feeder was completely ignored, its first customers showed up, house finches, the females drab and brown, the males spruce in their new fall plumage, streaked bodies, red crown and breast. Soon too, little Oregon juncos began to arrive, handsome birds, with a black hood covering head and shoulders, pink sides, a chestnut back, and a black tail with white outer tail feathers. With them came white-crowned and golden-crowned sparrows, bold and scrappy song sparrows, shy and gentle fox sparrows.

Once our feeder was operating at full speed, with often a hundred or more birds spread out across the driveway picking up scattered seeds, other eyes than ours began to notice the concentration. One day while I was at work, my wife heard a commotion at the feeder as all the birds flew up in a panic. She rushed to the window to see a gray and black bird, scarcely larger than the finches and sparrows themselves, that had darted into the midst of the birds and grabbed a tiny junco and bitten it through the skull. It was a shrike—a song-bird which has developed a hooked beak and predatory habits. It struggled up into a bush carrying the junco—almost as big as it was—in its bill. It hopped clumsily through the branches with its unwieldly burden till it got to the far side, and then, hawk-like, seized the bird in its claws, and flew off across the fields, barely able to keep its altitude it was so weighted down.

Within a few minutes the other birds, which had dived into bushes, flown under the porch, or into the garage, reappeared and went on feeding, ignoring the tiny puff of black and white tail feathers on the ground next to them.

Not many days later we heard the birds fly up again, some actually banging against the glass of the kitchen window in their panic. When we looked out, a slender, exquisite little sharp-shinned hawk had landed on the ground, not ten feet away, walking round and round the bird he had killed, his bright red eye glittering, his long tail jerking up and down with excitement. Another time a merlin, a small, swift-flying, scimitar-winged falcon, swept by the house and scooped up one of our birds on the wing, overtaking the frantically flying bird as if it had been standing still.

This no doubt seems cruel to some, but it is the way nature operates, the predators cutting back the overproduction of small birds, or working around the edges, clearing out injured or sick which would otherwise starve slowly, or perhaps spread disease to their fellows. In our misguided kindness we would kill off all the big birds to save the little ones (as if only the little ones have a right to live) and in the end snap the intricate threads by which all these creatures are connected.

It is another instance where nature is "kinder" than we are. For my own part, I must say the fine big raptors, as bird watchers call them (from the Latin for 'plunderer'), are my favorites among the birds, and I do not begrudge them a few of my juncos for the sake of seeing their fine outline, their tremendous flight. I am simply raising the concept of bird feeder to a higher power.

By this time autumn was well advanced and turning insensibly into winter. Geese honked overhead, and I ran out of my study to see them, snow geese, white birds with black wingtips, heading south for their wintering grounds on Skagit Bay. Our own bay out in front was filled almost from shore to shore with rafts of ducks running into several thousands, wigeon, pintails, mallard, teal, tiny black and white bufflehead, stocky black scoters, nearly white oldsquaw and goldeneye. Farther offshore three to four thousand black brant (a small, arctic-breeding goose) sat quietly, waiting for a nighttime low tide, so they could come in and gorge on eel grass without the hunters molesting them. The eagles were regular now, as many as five at once sitting on the tree out front, sometimes waking us up first thing in the morning with their surprisingly puny whimpering little call.

On the flat agricultural land adjoining the island, a number of other northern raptors had moved down into the area: brown, day-flying short-eared owls sat seemingly on every fence post, twitching their heads all the way around to watch us with staring yellow eyes as we drove past. Marsh hawks coursed through the fields, flying rapidly and low over the ground, hoping to surprise a mouse out of its burrow. Occasionally we would see the pere-grine falcon, here in his last stronghold (persistent pesticides have exterminated him over most of the United States). This is one of the most exciting birds, with its huge eyes and heavy black mustaches (or sideburns) coming down the sides of the face, a sort of pure essence of the predatory. Peregrines diving at their prey are thought to reach speeds well over 200 miles per hour, and they strike with so much impact that their victims' bones are sometimes shattered and knocked outside their skin.

One special day I was driving home from work along the flats when I looked, blinked, and looked again. On fence posts near the road were sitting two enormous, pure white owls. I stopped and looked at them stupidly, and they looked stupidly back at me. Snowy owls, right out of a White Owl cigar ad.

And now the snow came, only five or six inches, but followed by a cold snap, the temperature not rising above freezing for two or three weeks, making it impossible for small birds to forage on the ground, since the ground had a frozen shield over it. We shoveled the snow off fallen apples, put out pounds of bird-seed, suet, scraps from left-over dinner meat, left-over frostings and cakes (for the rich sugar content), homemade bread, nuts, stale cheese, and the birds came in droves. One sad day we watched a barn owl—a bird which usually hunts at night—out in the broad daylight flying low over the ground and diving repeatedly into the snow. He could hear the mice running in their tunnels a few inches under the snow, but he couldn't get at them. The next spring we found the body of a barn owl lying in the grass where it had died of starvation, its body so emaciated it had not even rotted, but was dried out a perfect mummy.

But by late February the air has already noticeably softened. It is wet and cool, but there is a feeling of life in it. Willow catkins are out, perhaps the first fool-hardy bulbs are poking through the dead leaves. I suspect everyone watches for the first signs of spring, but if you are a birdwatcher, you walk about in this season with your ears tuned to catch the first birdsong. Perhaps if the sun comes out from the clouds and shines with small but sensible warmth, one of the song sparrows in the bramble thickets will begin tuning up, two introductory notes, and then a long improvisation of trills and runs. In deepest woods the thumb-sized winter wren will send out an astonishing cascade of melody. The juncos will begin, from the top of some tree, their weak monotonous rattle.

And then—and this is what the bird watcher has really been listening for, the first real sign of spring—one day along in early March there will be a song almost like the rattle of the junco, but with a change at the end. Not very fancy, but it will be the first warbler of the year.

Warblers are amazing, and only bird watchers ever get to see them. They are tiny, quick, active, brightly colored birds, their intricate patterns running to yellows and blacks and whites, and they sing constantly as they forage through the woods, searching under every leaf, every curled back bit of bark, every matted bough of fir or cedar, for the tiny insects they feed on. In the spring migration they pass through in enormous noisy numbers, but for all that they are surprisingly inconspicuous, usually slipping all but invisibly through the topmost branches of tall trees. The different species would be nearly impossible to identify, if it wasn't for their songs. But fortunately they sing, and with a little practice, and very great delight, the different songs can be learned so well that you can identify a warbler from as far away as sound travels, and sometimes when you get back from a bird walk and jot down the different species you have encountered, it is hard to remember whether you have actually seen them, or merely heard them, the experience has been so strong either way.

If winter birding is done by eye, scanning the mudflats for waterfowl, the open country for raptors, spring and early summer birding is done by ear. I sometimes sit working in my study with the door open to let in sounds from outside, and it is as good as a three-dimensional walk in the woods, for I can hear constantly the buzz chatter click of passing swallows, and visualize their swift twisting flight; or a crisp buh-doop buh-dee from a nearby tree, and see in my mind's eye the red head, bright yellow body, black wings of a western tanager. The different warblers are calling in the fruit trees outside, or in the thickets along the cliff edge, the weary buzz of an orange-crown, the bright notes of a yellow, the wheeze of a black-throated gray; from the top of a tree out front a Bewick's wren, not much bigger than a bumble bee, is splitting my ears with his ee-you PLINK PLINK PLINK. From far off the haunting fluted notes of a Swainson's thrush, rising and rising until they are pitched almost out of hearing, then the tired note of a white- crowned sparrow.

The summer gets hotter and dryer, and the bird population is steady now, all of them busy raising families, no one moving about very much, so that even with all this plenty the ear gets jaded. We think if we have to wake up one more morning to all identically the same birds singing, we will go mad. It is, in short, the birdwatcher's summer doldrums.

But now the birds, so busy with their families, so hidden behind the dense thickets, stop singing, and there is a pall of silence which is even worse than the singing had got to be. But the season is moving all the time. The swallows who dependably came back and nested under the porch have raised two broods of greedy young and sent them packing. Young spotted-breasted robins are hopping tentatively across the lawn, trying to catch worms, new starlings in their brown first-year plumage have gathered into adolescent gangs of marauding hoodlums, and one day as we look out over the empty mud flats of Smiley Bay, we see what looks like an animated cloud of smoke, a white puff fifty feet high which changes shape and become fifty feet long instead, then bunches up into a tight circle and flashes bright silver, then turns black and stretches out in a long line, then twinkles white. We watch fascinated for half an hour. We are convinced believers in phantoms, fantasms, will-o'-the-wisps—except that, being birders, we know it is a precision-flying flock of a thousand tiny "peeps," little sandpipers who passed through here briefly in the spring, coming up from South America on their way up to the arctic to nest—but they can hardly have had a chance to raise a single fast-growing brood, and here they are turned around and coming back again, passing through on their way to Argentina, taking the coast all the way, living their lives in almost permanent migration, for when they get all the way down, they will have to turn right around, and come hurrying back up to be in time for next spring's nesting.

And fall comes earlier this time, because we know more about the birds, and are watching for them, and this time we see the sheltered corners of the bay fill up with drab brown ducks all looking like female mallards. They are in eclipse plumage, the drab non-breeding moult they go into in late summer, but observing them closely through the spotting scope, we can already see the faint traces of the bright green heads the drake mallards will soon put on, the rufous sides, and bald pate of the wigeon, the white streaks running up the sides of the necks of the pintails.

And can it be so soon! We hear cuc-cuc-cuc and then a mani-acal echoing laugh, and the two dozen loons are there, in their bright polka-dot and black pattern, laughing at us, are they? because the year has gone, but no time has gone, it is not the new year, it is the same year again, and we see how oriental we have gotten, how circular, as year repeats year, and soon again my work will be interrupted by a loud honking outside, and I will run out of my study to see V's of snowgeese overhead, perfect white bodies and shining black wingtips, and we will wake in the morning to the puny and foolish giggling of eagles in the tree out front, and begin unconsciously watching for the first peregrine, the first snowy owl, listening, yes listening, way in the background, for the first warbler of spring, seeking the first nest of summer, the first smoke cloud of acrobatic peeps in the fall.

And indeed for all our circular sense of time, our bodies are still progressing towards decay and death. The seasons fly all the faster when we begin to believe in our own mortality, and the loons laugh the more maniacally, for they are the changeless background against which we measure our change, the loons who swam alongside *Hespornis* and will swim alongside whatever comes into being after our hopeless race is gone. Nature herself has pushed more species into extinction than we, with our super-tankers and misplaced sentimentality, ever can—it is how she operates. But the species remaining she diversifies, till they fill every niche, become all the species all over again in a new and equally wonderful way, endlessly inventive, procreative. *Hespornis*, the dinosaurs, man too, have all had a fair chance, it just happens we were not made so perfectly as the loon, and so we fall aside, but our little failures are not very important. We alone pass on. The seasons return.[10]

[10]THIS TO MUCH NICE POEM   I TAKED IT TO MY POETRY GROUP TO SHARE   I TRYED TO TRANSLATE IT TO NOW/LANG BUT TO HARD   THE LANG NOT HARD THO   WE CAN NOT OF CORSE RECOVER EACH SOUND AN HOW IT SOUNDED TO THEN/TIME MAN AN LITTEL DIFF'S IN HOW A WORD MEANS   BUT MOST HARD WAS TO CATCH BACK TIME WHEN MANI BUGS LIKE "warblers" FLYED ABOUT AN MAKED THERE SOUND AN GOED SHIT ON THE GROUND   ("guano")

BUT WE CAN SHARE THE FORM   WHICH VERI GUD HERE   HOW THE "loons" (A KIND OF BUG THAT LIVED IN WATER)   COME AT THE START OF POEM ONLI AS BUGS   BUT COME BACK AT END AS MORE THEN BUGS   AS SINE OF TIME/STILL   VS   TIME/MOVING   AS SINE IN GENERAL OF ALL THEN/TIME'S HISTORI VS   WHAT?

I BE TEMTED TO SAI HE ALMOST SEE TO WE'S TIME OF POST/HISTORI

BUT IN FACT HE MERELY NOT CORRECT   "loons" BE HERE FOR ALL TIME ON MIKE-TAPE   MAN HAD TO CHOOSE   EITHER THE LIFE SEEN IN POEM   WHERE MAN GOED AN BUGS   ANIMALS   STAYED   OR LIFE WHERE MAN STAYED AN BUGS GOED

HIS WAY MAKE FOR NICE POEM   SAD   "romantic"   BUT NOT MAKE FOR REEL LIFE

MAIBI HE UNDERSTANDED THAT

STILL   THIS TO MUCH NICE POEM

[Here's another fragment, in Davie's hand, that I don't know quite what to do with. The first part is missing, so there's no date or place, but, though they seem to feel they are coasting a large island, it can only be some part of Australia, which was known then as New Holland, and whose geography was, at that time, imperfectly known, as Cook hadn't sailed around it yet. For an expedition ostensibly searching for a northwest passage around North America, they certainly were spending a lot of time in the South Seas, but I suspect they were also a voyage of general discovery, and perhaps doing some navigational work: other fragments, too brief and scattered to be worth including here, mention such things as "transeckting *Venus*" etc., all pretty far over the present editor's head.

Although, as I say, I believe in this section they are coasting aboriginal Australia, they might just as well have got into a science-fiction time warp, and caught a straight glimpse into the Pleistocene.]

for 41 Dais along the Barren *Shoar*, flat, dry Yellow Grass-land, inland shimmering wt Heat, distant Mountaynes rising & wriggling, cleaving in Two in the heat shimmer, & sometimes reproducing themselvs upside-down right above theire Real Selves, & no sign of *humayne* Habitation, & never once a *River* curving thro' the *Playnes* & coming out to *Sea*, where we cou'd find Sweet Water, wch we was grown short of, our *Casks* rank & briny & distastefull.

At length on the scrubbie grassie Land uprose an Island of dustie grey-blew *Gum* Trees, hard & crustie, but wch we hop'd betockend Water, & we down Anchor. Dr *Harris*, & I, was uneasie at the look of the High Surf, but was eager to Sett Foot on this Straunge *Land* & see what Natural Producktions it offer'd, so when the *Boys* said they thou't they cou'd get the *Long-Boat* safely thro', we jin'd em, for a perilous *Journey* wich made me dredd the return *Journey* to the *Shipp*, & Dr *Harris*, said the same.

But then I wou'd not for the *World* have misst our Adventure. No breath of Wind ashoar, as tho' the very *Ayr* had lost Hart in this searing *Land*, & lay listless & dying on the Parcht *Erth*. Giant

Cicadas sang everywhere, some in shrill Whisles, tothers Clancking like Iron beat with a Hammer, near deafning in the else Stillness. We lookt up to see a vast *Eagle* with a Diamond-shap'd Tayle soaring above us, well out of Range of our *Guns*.

We scoutid In-Land, & found to our Deleight, a *Spring* upwelling, fresh & cold, into what appar'd to be an artificially dugg out Mud-Wall'd *Pond*. 100s of green *Paroquets* flew up with a grate Clammour, to smal for Food, but we took a Brayce for Speciments.

The *Boys wou'd need several Tripps to the Shipp* to replenish all our Casks, for they cou'd not get thro' the Surf if they was too Loaden, & it was slowe Work filling em 1 & by 1 in the small *Pond*, so whilst they begin rolling up Tuns from the *Beech*, Dr *Harris*, & I, took us a Jar of Water, a Sack of *Bisketts*, our *Guns* & sett out In-Land.

We walkt for 3 *Howres*, ascending a gently rising *Skarp*, seeing very Little, occasionally flushing small *Birds* from the Grass, but never managing to take any. We did colleck a very odd *Lizzard* like Creatur, armourd & be-spin'd, wch had this curious propetty, that it's round flat *Tayle* exactly mirrour'd it's round flat *Head*, so 't was impossible, at a Glance, to kno' wch way it went. 't Was indeed so Lethargic, it little matter'd.

But then, & I suspeck we was some 10 *Miles* In-Land, we saw what at 1st we took to be a Storm of Dust ahead, (indeed, a hot blast of *Ayr* had begun to Blo',) & then heard Crackling, & wth alarm realiz'd 't was a raging Grass*fire*. We commenc't to fear for our Safety, for the scortching *Wind* must carry the Flames right on us, but when we climb'd what appar'd a Knole before us, the better to ascertayne our Situation, to our Astonishment a precipitous *Gorge* plummitid a 100 ft to the dry wash of a *River* Bedd direckly below us. 't Was perhaps a 100 ft Wide as well, & gowg'd right out of the *Playne*, for the far *Bank* rose up in a similar perpendickular Wall, to be on a level with us acrost the *Chasm*. Indeed we had not been able to see the *Gorge*, intill we stood right at its Edg. To our Relief now we realiz'd the spindley

Grass flames cou'd not reech acrost this natural *Barrier*, & we sat ourself's down to watch the developpment of the Wild-Fire, at least intil such *Time* as the Smoak drove us Back. After a while above the Cracklin Sound of the flames, we heard a powerful drumming, as of *Hoof-Beats*, & at once the intire *Playne* came to life with 100s & 100s of a Giant Monstrous Misshapen *Beest*, racing in Terrour, *Donkey*-Like heads & Ears, tiny little *Humayne* Hands & Arms clutcht to thzre *Brests*, rar'd up on theire hinder Legs & long thick *Tayles*, & leaping along on these hinder Leggs with inmense Speed & Power, such as cou'd o'ertake the fastist *Horse* or *Grey-Hound*. They was outdistancing the Flames, but we saw they must soon face an equal Daunger, if they mayntayn'd theire Coarse, of dashing themselvs to Death of[f] the *Clift*. At any Moment now, I remarckt to Dr *Harris*, they must surely swerve to one side, & race along the *Clift* Edg, if they wou'd avoyde Disaster. But just then, Dr *Harris*, took my Arm, & poynted below: *The River Bedd had come alive with Humayne Beeings!*

If such *Creaturs* cou'd be so Christn'd, hirsute & running in a croutching shambling Gayte, heavie Brow'd & calling 1 tother with piercing *Bird* whisles, carrying Clubbs & long poynted Sticks for Weapons, & with wiry yellow *Dogs* ranging feral & salvage looking, just before em. There was perhaps 10 of em al together, & they back'd against the Wall direckly below us, so we had to crane out to look down on em, & they was wayting, obviously at the highest Pitch of Excitement, for what then Transpir'd.

For now we lookt back to the Panicking *Creaturs* outrunning the Flames. They came up near, *Eys* rolling, *Tongues* out & *Mowths* Foaming, & wth ne'er the least thou't of swerving, or checking theire *Pace*, they shott out o'er the Clift, plung'd in a continuing *wave* to the sharp Rocks below, where they was dasht all to Pieces, a sickning thudding Sound, & where succeeding *Wave* after *Wave* continu'd plunging over, & crashing down on those already below. The slouhter was gastly to us, but yet it went on, & then it went on. There was now so high a pile of dasht-to Death *Corses*, that those still falling, had a softer Bedd to land on, & was not kill'd outright, but onelie Maimd, & Twitcht & Scream'd, till enough of theire Fellows falling on em from Above finisht em, or at least burie'd em. I think it may have taken a Quarter of an *Howre*, tho' it seem'd to us an *Age*, before the last fell, floating down & down endlesslie, before smashing, Many of the latist falln were bleating & thrashing abowte. The Line of *Flame* had come to the *Clift* Edg now, & sent a hot Breath of Smoak & Cinders towrds us.

Below, the *Men*, now certayne no mor wou'd come plunging down on em, ran forward, & dragg'd of[f] 7 of the big *Creaturs*, & disembowl'd em, & flea'd off theire *Hydes*, in a very short *Time*, tho' using onelie sharpen'd Sticks, & *Knife* Blaydes of Wood, & then wth a kind of *Ax*'s, cut these 7 Bodies up into smaller Peices of *Flesh*, wch they wrappt in peices of the *Hydes*, & hoistid on theire Backs. Now we saw 4 of theire *Fellows* standing on top of the *Clift* Edg opposite us, where the Fire had maynely burnt itself out, & they was jibbering down to those below, & jumping up & down wth Pleasure. One lookt at us for a long *Moment*, then, as if refusing to credit his *Senses*, he rejoynd the others & ne'er glanc't our Waye Agayne. They gestur'd down *Stream*, to where they apparentlie said they wou'd jine theire *Comrades*, & then sett out that way at a Trott, whilst those below, theire burdens shou'der'd, walkt off in that direcktion to jine em.

I lookt at Dr *Harris*, who lookt at me. They must have *sett* the Fire, I said, suddaynly realizing it myself. He nodded slowly; I make out, said I, they kill'd 1,500 of the *Beasts* in order to carry off those 7. Do ye still mayntayne, in the face of this, that *Man* is a 'Noble Salvage', become debaucht & brutaliz'd onelie as he has become more *Civiliz'd*, or must ye Grant now, that ther has been at least Some developpment & progress from our *Ab-Originals*? Dr *Harris*, lookt Ashen, & made no reply.

To our Surprise, when we return'd to the *Spring*, ther was a *Family* of these *People* standing Gawking at the *Boys* who was talking to em Chearfully, as tho' they cou'd understand. Ther was a *Man* of abt Middle Age, his *Wife*, looking very Old, & perhaps a 2d *Wife*, carrying a *Babe*, but looking very Yong, perhaps just arriv'd of *Child* baring Age, & another *Child*, of 3 or 4 yrs. The *Boys* had givn the *Man*, & the old *Womman*, & the yong *Womman*, Pipes to Smoak, & they was injoying em. They all had writ on theire *Faces* a Look of Child-Like Wonderment at these Straungers in theire Midst, but nothing of Fear or Hostility. The *Man*, from up Cloase, was almost Handsome, thick beardid & shaggy Hair'd, & short in Stature, but very strongly made, & a dark rich coppery Coulour. The old *Womman* was falln in the *Duggs*, & like the *Man* stark Nakkid, but lookt quite Hale & Chearfull, & was bak't quite Black by the Sun. The Yong *Wife*, hareless & smooth Skinn'd, had barely enough *Bosom* to give Suck. She had a Pett of 1 of the green *Paroquets*, & smil'd, toying wt it, & had fine strong white Teeth.

Yer can f.ck the Yong un if yer likes, 1 of the *Boys* said to us as we came up. The old *Man* dont mind a Fart, he just Grins. She arn't Bewtifull, but tis better nor frigging in yer Hand. *Christie* is waitin for yers to have a Go if yer likes, fore he has his, so yers wont cotch his Clap.

[Here is another fragment from the South Seas, also in Davie's hand.]

told us that unlike the Others, from whom we might have some profitable Trayde, (more especially, they meant, abowte theire *Fort*, where we must pay Custom,) there was a silly, dreamie gaggle of *Peresoso*'s, or Lazys, careing for nothing more then theire *Prohas*, or *Boats*, in wich they was forever making fantastickal journies to no Purpose, but as theire *Island* lay in our Waye, & as the Arrogant & Condescending *Govournour* of the Spanish *Fort*, as grasping & greedie & *groat* pinching a Shopp Keeper *Govournour* as ye shall ever see, had mayde but a sowre Impression upon us, our Curiosity was piqu'd to see em, & theire *Prohas*, wich had a Fame all abowte the *World*.

We came upon it from the East, or high, Side, where it was regularly beat by the strong Seas from the Steddy *Trades*, but circling round it, we Anchor'd on the shelter'd West-side, abowte 1 *Mile* from *Shoar*, a flatt, low *Land*, full of Sandy *Bayes*. A number of theire *Boats* had come out to meet us, & indeed they was a Miracle to see, cutting the Waves wt a Dazzling Pace. They was a sort of dubbel-bow'd Dugg-out *Canoa*, onelie wt a 2d *Hull* riding out several *Feet* to 1 *Side*, & parallel to the Main *Hull*, the 2 *Hulls* conneckted by 12 *inch* diameter bamboo Poles lasht fore & Aft. The 2d, or Out-Riding *Hull*, was more slender, & not dugg out for *Men* to ride in, but appar'd to give Ballance onelie. The *Boats* had a single *Mast* in the Centre, wt a long Mizzin-like *Yard*, made fast to the front of the *Boat*, tother End hanging over the *Sterne*. Altho' we was Crowding Sayle, they passt us as like we was at Anchor, laughing in good- Natur'd deleight wt theire own Prowess. One *Boat* pull'd along-side, & a *Man* within shoutid up to us, in *Spanish*, for a Line, wch we tosst him, & he scrambl'd up it in a trice, & scrambl'd Aboard, a Handsome & Muscular Copper-skinn'd *Indian*, tall & straight, who solemplie shook the Hand of all who was standing near, then explayn'd in pretty good *Spanish*, that he shou'd be our *Pilot*. He led us to a pretty good, shelter'd Anchorage, as I describ'd befor, all the Whyle tactfully & discreetlie looking abowte him at our *Shipp*, wich was evidentlie of Intrest to him, for he had ne'er befor seen an English *Shipp*. Altho' a young *Man*, he had abowte him a something dignifi'd, as tho' he were an important *Man* amongst his People, & accustom'd to receiving Respeck; & indeed, tho' the *Boys* are often enough *Rascals* & readdy to fleer at Straungers & Condescend to the *Salvages*, they was quiet & well behav'd.

Mr *Mountague*, presentid him as a Gift, wt a fine steel *Ax*, wch he examin'd politely, feeling the Edg, & the ballance, & then politely handid it back to the Captain, not understanding it was meant him to have. Mr *Mountague*, smil'd, & said, severall Times, *Presento Presento*, at wch he at length understanding, once more shook all our Hands agayne.

A grate many of the *Indians* had climb'd aboard by now, all tall
& comely & dignifi'd, as they toucht nothing, but walkt around,
examining the *Shipp* very discreetlie. None carri'd *Weapons* of
any Sort, & all was seemlie Dress'd in a sort of Hempen *Skirt*
abowte the *Loynes* & down to the *Knees*. Theire very gracious
Politeness won our Favour, & the *Boys* quicklie invitid em down
into the *Shipp* to see, & we all had open Howse in all our Rooms,
& gave em free Run, for we cou'd see they was not, as some other
Indians we had unfortunately had to do wt, inclin'd to be
Thievish.

Now we droppt our *Long-boats*, & they escorted us Ashoar,
where a grate Feast was preparing for us, of sweet *Co- Co Nuts*,
some *Rice, Pine Appels, Water-Melons, Oranges, Limes*, &
Bread-Fruits, wich they pick from the Trees like *Appels*, & wich
are the bigness & consistencie of a Penny Loaf. Also we had *Fish*,
& *Hoggs* roasted in theire Skins. The *People* was most gentle &
seemlie in all theire Motions, & mighty generous to us, constantly watching to see we had this or that to sup or drink, & a
steady traffick of *canoas* went out to those of our *Men* still on the
Shipp, carrying em victuals to eat, & excess to stoar below Decks.
Tho' theire Oeconomy was but simple, the *Island* was smiling, &
suppli'd all needs wt but a Minimum of Labour, & the *Natives*,
tho' in no respeck Lazy or Slothfull or Filthy, seem'd content but
to have of what *Nature* suppli'd so bounteously, for we saw no
Signs of intensive Cultivation, but onelie each simple Grassy
Howse, wt no Walls, but onelie upright Poles & a Thatch Roof
had round it plantid, a *Lime* or *Orange* or *Bannano* Tree, a Patch
of *Melons*, & in low places, *Rice* Sprouts was plantid. *Pigs* ran
Wilde abowte, & little Nakkid *Childern*. Theire was no Mess or
Nastiness abowte, & also, (to the *Boys* disappoyntment!), no
woemmen was anywhere to be seen, wether thro' Modestie, or
thro' Jealousy of us on the part of theire *Husbands*[11]

We was made the more aware, by the Deference pay'd him,
that our *Pilot* was a *Man* of *Note*, & we thou't perhaps he was a
Prince or so, but in observing em, we at length cou'd not discover

one who appar'd to be the *King*, nor indeed anything wich cou'd properly be denominatid an Hyerarchy, for each *Man* seem'd to dispose things for himself, wt no one ordering him (tho' ther was no bickering or quarreling niether), in what wou'd be a perfeck equalitie of *Democracie*, but that, as I have remarckt, our *Pilot*, & some Dozen others, seemd marckt out for special Deference, & tho' they did not Lord it o'er the others, but comportid themselvs wt almost more Modestie, they obviously expecktid the Deference as theire Dew. Nor did these seem partickular Giants in Stature, as if a *Warrior* Caste, & indeed we had not, nor did we ever, see any sign of what cou'd be call'd a Weapon on the intire *Island*, save onelie some fine long *Fish* Speers.

At length, we askt our *Piloto*, who knew the *Spanish* Tongue, who these men cou'd be, & poynted out to him these Special *Men*, & he smil'd, & said they was the "Navegadores", or, Navigators, & wt grate dignitie, he poynted to himself, & said "Yo Tambyen", that is to say, "So am I too". He then explain'd to us, that theire grate *Wati-Wati*, wich I take to be theire *God*, had given em all things out of the *Erth* & the *Sea*, so they needed not to struggle or fight amongst themselvs for possessions, for all was own'd in Common, save onelie theire partickular *Wives*, & even theire *Childern* was rais'd by the *Communitie*, so that all liv'd in Peace & perfeck Equality, wt no *Man* higher then Another, for they believ'd they was in fack all 1 single *Family*. Since theire was no War, none could'd be singl'd out as *Warriors*, & since ther was no ownershipp, none cou'd be singl'd out for Wealth, & since they was but 1 *Family*, none cou'd be a *Nobilitie* above the Rest;

¹¹"Woemmen" = MAN W/ BABI-CARRING PARTS   THEN/TIME MAN THINK THER BE 2 KINDS: "man" = MAN W/ CUM/COCK   "woman" = MAN W/ BABI/HOLE   BECUZ THEN/TIME MAN THINK THIS THER BE MUCH SILLI/SAD TRUBBEL   FOR EGSAMP: "man" MORE BETTER THAN "woman"   SO   "man"   CAN   BE   GUV   CAN   BE   THINK/ TEACH   THINK/TECH   ECT BUT NOT "woman"   "woman" CAN PLAY W/ BABI   CAN MAKE COOK   CAN MAKE RED LIPS   "man" NOT MOST SILLIEST: "man" CAN ONLI FUK "woman"   NOT LIKE WE ALL MAKE HAPPI LUV/LUV

but ther was borne amongst em, certayne who from earliest *Yeers* was markt out by a special Calling, to become *Navigadores*, & these learnt all the *Sea-Wuyes*, & held in theire *Heads*, the Picture of the *Skies* over any Place in the *Ocean*, & these glori'd in taking long Voyages, in theire *Prohas*, to all the wide-flung *Islands*, scatter'd like grains of *Rice* (as he put it) o'er the vast Trackts of *Sea*, on wich theire *People*, from Earlie *Dayes*, had settl'd, & now kep in Contack onelie by these Journies, guided by the *Naviga-dores*, who contayn'd in theire living Memories, the knowledge of where each *Island* & *Village* was, over a 1,000 *Leagues* & more of *Sea*. This Knowlidge was in effeck theire culture, or theire Literature, & the *Navi*-gadores stood in a place betwixt a *Priest* & a *Bard*.

On our 2d *Daye* Ashoar, ther was grate shouting & chattring & excitment & our *Piloto* inform'd us, wt Tears of Emotion in his *Face*, that indeed this very *Daye* theire *Brothers* from a far distant *Isle* was arriving, had been remarckt from a *Headland*, & in abowte 2 *Howres*, a grate Flotilla of their *Prohas* escortid in a *Proha* wt a slightlie diffrent Desseign paintid on its *Sayle*, & 7 Smiling *Men* Walkt somewhat stiffly out of the *Boat*, & imbrac'd those greeting em on the *Beech*, & then all turn'd to watch the *Navigador* rise shakily from the *Tiller*, a look of Payne on his face, tho' he was grinning, heavy black Lines under his *Eys*, his Eys weary & Bloodshot, holding his hand to shield em from the Sun, wich irritatid em so they drippt wt Tears. He cannot sleep on the intire Journie, the *Piloto* told us, for if he cloas'd his Eys even for a short Time, he wou'd lose Track of where they were.

Ther now commenc't a new *Daye* of Feesting & Rejoyceing, for the visiting *Heroes*, & we realiz'd the feesting we had had, was not simplie Welcome to a *Guest*, but rather meant Honour to us also as long-distance *Mariners*, & we felt a sudden Flush of Pride in this our

[The fragment breaks off.]

[By this time I think we might almost fill in some of the rest. I don't know where the good captain might stand on these people, but I can imagine Dr. Harris's dry comments to Davie about how "backwards" and barbaric these people are, except for the few living around the Spanish fort who have "developed" and "progressed" into money grubbing traders, like all good modern civilized people. I suppose I hold to some sort of middle ground. I guess I don't much believe in Dr. Harris's "noble savage" anymore than I believe in Davie's constant sort of Darwinian progress. Both have things to be said for them, but at one end of the scale is "Pleistocene overkill" and at the other genocidal war. It seems to me that a given culture, certainly, can correct or corrupt, and that technology does run on linearly, constantly changing all the givens. But I'm not sure that man himself changes at all, for common threads seem to run through the whole story: "We are in a depression here. A stark place... pockmarked by craters... the sky is completely black...." This is the voice of the astronauts, who, as a good liberal, I ought to be opposing since they are wasting wealth that could be feeding starving people, or displacing our attention from earth-bound ills, but I hear in the excited, the enthusiastic tones, the voice of an older traveler: "There we saw a cave on the verge, close to the sea high up, overhung with laurel. Many animals usually slept there, sheep and goats; a courtyard was built high around it out of deep-bedded stones and tall pines and oak trees with lofty foliage. There a monstrous man usually slept, who alone and aloof tended the animals. He did not consort with the others, but stayed apart and had a lawless mind. And indeed he was formed as a monstrous wonder. He looked not like a grain-eating man but like a wooded crest on lofty mountains that appears singled out from the others." This is Odysseus, leading his men straight into a hopeless trap locked up in the cave of the Cyclops, who killed and ate several of them before Odysseus, the man who was never at a loss, devised a clever revenge and escape, to his greater glory, though that glory cost him half a dozen of his

[52]

best fighters. I don't mean I condone Odysseus's selfish action—
what is the point of judgment? I am merely describing the human
spirit. We all die soon enough, but beforehand if we want, we can
see a lot of things, experience a lot of things, always with those
same accents of excitement. Not just in making wide-ranging
journeys. "You can have psychological adventures," a pallid and
slender student once remarked to me, saying why he was able to
identify with adventurers of the more usual cast. "I have traveled
much in Concord," quoth Thoreau, and Gilbert White, the
18th-century inventor of scientific field ornithology (for this and
other reasons my personal hero), who never left his beloved
parish of Selborne, but traveled deeply within it, gave it as his
opinion "that if ftationary men would pay fome attention to the
diftricts on which they refide, and would publifh their thoughts
refpecting the objects that furround them, from fuch materials
might be drawn the moft complete country-hiftories... [yet even
failing this] there remains this confolation behind—that thefe his
purfuits, by keeping the body and mind employed, have, under
Providence, contributed much health and cheerfulnefs of fpirits,
even to old age."]

* * *

He looked up from the typewriter, and the activity of the
house returned to him. Marina was sitting on her "island" in a
ray of warm sun, preening and occasionally turning to snap her
mandibles at an annoying fly. J was in the front room working on
her grebe painting, and had the radio going. She needed the radio
going while she worked; he liked complete silence. But the radio
only really bothered him when his work was going badly, for he
tended to listen to it rather than concentrating, and if she turned
it very low, he only strained his ears the harder to hear it. Idly, he
trapped the fly against the window and caught it in his fingers,

[53]

and carried it into the front room and put it in Guinevere's jar. J had completed a very promising pencil drawing of the grebe, just the head and long white swan-like neck, and next to it, the very complicated lobed foot. She had painted in the red eye so far, and was working on the long yellow bill, which was coming out quite successfully round and tactile.

"Going pretty good," he said.

"I think so too. The bill's taken all morning. What're you going to do now?"

"I have to go to the unemployment office to pick up my check."

She went into the kitchen and put on a saucepan of milk for their morning coffee, made half with milk in the British fashion. The radio as always was tuned to the Canadian station, the CBC, modelled after the BBC. Ben Metcalf, the top Canadian journalist, came on for his regular commentary. The Third World War, he said, has already started, and is well named, for it is a war of attrition of the third world, through encroaching Saharas, changing climate, imperialism, the western countries slowly getting control of all food production, while quickly using up the resources of the developing countries before they have enough technology to use them for themselves.

They took the coffees out to the back lawn, and sat down on the sleeping bag out in the full sun.

J watched him sympathetically, knowing the argument was continuing in his head.

"He's absolutely right," George finally said. "If the West survives at all, it will only be with a hideous burden of guilt at having survived at everyone else's expense."

"What should we do?" J asked. He found her looking at him earnestly, and suddenly felt a bit false, and saw that all the arguments, though he believed them, he had removed to a comfortable abstraction.

"I guess there's no answer. I guess we must only realize how privileged we are to live in this moment of history, and to be right

[54]

here at a point where technology has made our lives safe and easy, and yet some of the natural world remains. Even if things go out of control quickly, and our lives end badly, we have at least had all this. I don't see how the next generation can expect to have our luck."

Although he had not intended it, he realized this last had turned out to be another dart at her in their continuing, but in the main unspoken, or indirect, debate. Her rebuttal, though unspoken, was pretty direct.

The nearest house was across a vacant field from them which was overgrown with tall grass, concealing them from view if they stayed low. J stripped off her clothes to lie naked in the sun next to him, and he lay on one side next to her admiring her body shining with perspiration while the sun warmed his back, and just at the moment when he most wished she would she reached over, smiling, and began to undo his belt.

"I'm just being used," he said. "We're nothing but blind forces in the flow of history."

"Do you mind?" she said.

"Nope."

*   *   *

[This little scrap, written in the Dr.'s hand, can as well go here as anywhere:]

Very lazy Dais in the Steddy *Traydes*, the *Boyes* satt in the Sun all Daye this Daye mending & darning. For a Diversion some Wagg startid a Contention that *Jemmie* cou'd out-Clamber the *Mess-Boy*, & in a twinckling small Wagers was layd a both Sides, & a derring-do Contest was underway betwixt em. Both *Jemmie* & the *Mess-Boy* are small in Stature but like *Monkies* in the Yards, & not to bee outdone by anny in Daring. The *Boyes* hoop'd &

hollo'd to urge em on to anny Foolhardinesse, but I confess my *Hart* misgave to see em Walk Upreight on the Mizzin Sky Sayle 80 *Feet* above the *Decks*. Mr *Mountague*, then very sensible declar'd a Draw, & calld the *Boyes* doun, & all good-naturdlie declard it was a proper Ending, tho' believing there oun *Champioun* might have had the Edg. I was so pleas'd (maynely to see *Jemmi* back wt-out his Neck-Bone Broke) that I gave him a Silver *Croun*, wch hee acceptid wt delight, but also a bold Look into my *Ey*, wch quite put mee out of Countenance, & wich I kno' not now how to Interprett.

Butt in the Afternoon I went to my *Cabbin* for a Napp, warmd by the Sunn, & was swep awaye by Voluptuous *Dreems*, & woke in a sudden Fright that someone cou'd see or heer mee, butt of course I was alone. I felt my *Belly*, & it was Wett, &, 1st making certayne my Door was Fast, I friggd & friggd till no Dropp remaynd, butt still had no Peace, & the Lines kep repeeting themselvs in my Hedd

> *Bugger, bugger, bugger*
> *All in hugger-mugger*
> *Fire doth descend:*
> *'t Is too late to ammend*
> SODOM *Wilmot* Earl of *Rochestor*

* * *

Those who carry their whole village on their proa left us. We gave them half our pigs and all our breadfruit (God will give us more breadfruit in three changes of the moon), and followed them in our proas for part of the day. On the following day our brothers from far off Mari-titi left us, to visit more brothers and sisters.

We were very happy to see all these people, we had good

feasting and drank much rice beer and banana beer. When those who carry their whole village on their proa left us, we were happy for them that they would be traveling and seeing other islands, but we were sad to see them leave us. But in one respect it was pleasant, for they have no women in their village, so we had to hide our wives, to spare them the pain of remembering what they lacked, and that meant our wives could not share in the feasting and drinking, nor could we make love to them in the night.

So when they left, our wives came down out of the hills, and we had more feasting because we were happy that they had returned, and also because they had missed the first feasting, and we made love to our wives in the night.

But then the excitement was over, and everyone went back to whatever they were doing before, only I felt very restless, and I thought about all the other islands, and saw them in my mind, and saw the shape of the sky over them, and saw the sky circling at night, and I felt a craving to see the other islands, and to visit my brothers and sisters.

At night I made love to my wife, but she saw I was distant from her, and she said, Husband, you want to travel, and I said Wife, I think so. She went to sleep, but I lay awake, thinking about the shape of the sky, and I began to hear a sound in the night. It was the sound of coughing, the sound you make when you are swimming and accidentally swallow sea-water. It came from one house and then another, and at last I could hear coughing all around me, coughing and spitting. This was very strange, because, except when someone is swimming, this is a sound I never hear.

In the morning everyone could see that I wanted to travel, and all made way for me when I walked, and became quiet when I passed by. I could feel everyone watching me, and I pretended that I did not notice this, and joked with my sisters, and played with the children, so that I would not appear proud, though inside maybe I was a little bit proud. (Many of my brothers were still coughing, as if they had swallowed sea- water, or sneezing, as if they had smelled pepper, and their eyes watered and their noses ran, as if they had taken a large bite of roast pig when it was still too hot. It was very queer.)

I stayed away from the beach all day, and did not look toward where my proa was. One by one six of my young brothers came to me, and said, Brother, wherever you may be tomorrow, I would like to be with you.

Though I said nothing, the next morning, at the birth of the sun, when I went down to my proa, I found it loaded with food and water. The six brothers who had spoken to me were waiting there, their eyes full of excitement. Many of my brothers and sisters were on the beach, though a great many more were not. I pretended not to notice that many were absent. Those on the beach said, We have come to tell you how happy we are for you that you will be seeing other islands, but also we are sad to see you leave us. I said, I am honored that so many have come to see me off. I said that, so they would think I had not noticed how few had come. But they said, Naturally many more would like to have come, but—it is very queer—they do not feel right, they are coughing and spitting, and their eyes and noses are running, and they are stiff in all their muscles, and sore in their chests, and had to get up many times in the night to defecate, so now they are trying to sleep, but they also are happy for you, but sad for themselves that you are leaving.

We set out, and many of our brothers followed us in their proas for part of the day, but then smiling and waving to us, they turned back, and now we were truly traveling. When we are only going out a short way, to fish, or to meet and escort other travelers, there is less pleasure, for I always feel as if I am tethered to the island, like a pig tethered to a tree. I can go around, but I cannot go straight, there is a limit, and the limit pulls at me, my neck is always pulled slightly to one side by the tether I imagine that I feel.

But when we are truly going to travel, the tether is gone. I still feel restless when we are close to the island, and my brothers are still escorting us, although I am greatly honored that they love me enough to show me this honor, but at the moment they smile, and wave, and turn back, I feel my heart pound strongly, and my lungs expand, and I feel the happiness in my proa, for suddenly it feels that it is moving straight, that there is no more turn pulling its head to one side, and it darts forward like a fish spear, and my six brothers and I look at one another, and take one another's hands, and are too full for speech.

The first day's journey is familiar to all, the sea is our sea, it looks like the ground around our village, even the smallest child can find his way in it. I slept most of the day, and let the others guide the proa. A small while before the death of the sun, they woke me, and I looked where the sun was, and saw that the waves were still coming from the direction they come from near our island, and we still were in the sea around our village.

But then it was dark, and the stars again were free to travel in the sky. Now only I knew where we were. My brothers went to sleep, which is good, for I wanted no one talking or distracting me. (Only, one of my brothers was breathing loudly through his mouth, and each time he took in his breath, there was a catch in it, and then finally he had to cough to remove the catch.) I have to watch the stars circle, and remember the time, for when the time goes for a little bit, the stars turn a little bit, and then I must know to aim the proa at the new shape the sky makes. The waves continued to go the right way, but I kept watching them, and then there was a change, a different sound against the stern, a different feel to the rudder, and that meant we had the bigger waves that come between Mona-ratti and Kea-watti.

My one brother kept coughing, and got up three times to defecate over the side. He shook his head and apologized to me for disturbing me, but I joked with him to show him I was not disturbed, and told him he sounded like he had drunk too much banana beer.

Then I was concentrating, and I heard a lap against the sides, and the waves were smaller again, and had changed direction slightly, and that meant Kea-watti had come between us and the force of the great sea, and I must turn just the right amount, to avoid the reefs by Molo-itti.

When I relaxed again, I noticed that all my brothers were coughing, and because I felt sorry for them coughing, my own throat in sympathy began to have a catch in it, and I swallowed and swallowed, but finally, without meaning to, my breath ended with a little ripping cough.

Part of the circle of the sky went down behind the water, and the wind lightened. This meant the sea was beginning to prepare for the birth of the sun. Then there was a funny feeling in my stomach, which meant we were in the current which curls around behind the reefs of Molo-itti, and I turned a bit to correct for the current.

My brothers kept getting up to defecate over the sides, apologizing to me. I was coughing regularly now, and suddenly I felt a pain in my stomach, and very suddenly I had to squat back and defecate over the side right where I was sitting, and it came out like I had been drinking too much banana beer. I washed myself with the sea-water, and sat back down quickly, so that none of my brothers would notice, and when they got up, although I choked myself, I kept from coughing so they would not hear me cough.

A worry came to me: my stomach kept turning over and over, so how would I feel it when the reverse current comes which means we are past the reefs, and we must turn a certain amount, and then wait and feel carefully for the current to end, so that we can turn back again to pass around Mono-lotti? I watched the stars turning, and concentrated on the time.

But of course very soon the sky grew light, and the sun was born, and it is very easy to go by the sun, and the wave direction is easy to see, and it is easy to know the time. My mind must have been distracted that I forgot it was almost day.

We were all coughing now, and could hardly stop, and our eyes and our noses ran, and when we held the pieces of pig meat to our mouths, we quickly put them back down again, and knew

[60]

we would like nothing to eat. We each drank a bit of water, but even that made us feel funny.

It was funny what was happening to us, but we didn't have words to talk about it, so we talked about our new brothers and sisters that we would see in a few days, and after a while, we did not talk about anything, and my brothers tried to sleep some more, or just sat and looked at their feet.

Many times during the day I caught myself taking a little sleep, and woke with a jump, but I could see by the sun that only a little time had passed, and I had not taken my hand from the tiller. All my muscles felt swollen and sore, and I worried that the sun was moving so quickly to its death, for when night comes I must not take even a little sleep or I will not know how much time has gone. Now that we are past Mono-lotti, there is no more land but only the great sea for two days before we reach Kiri-ritti, where our closest brothers and sisters live. But it is by itself in the great sea with nothing beyond, so if we miss it we may not find anything again. Usually I am proud that I have the responsibility to find it, and that everyone trusts me to find it, because I know just where it is. But now I do not feel right, and I feel very weary, as if we had already been traveling more days instead of two days.

It is night, and my brothers are coughing and snorting in their sleep. We have only eaten a little dried dog-fish all day, and drunk too much water, so that it falls straight through us when we defecate, but our throats and our heads are on fire. Long rollers are coming across us from the great sea, the stars are circling, and I have the old feeling that the stars are still and that it is the proa, the world, the whole great sea itself, that is spinning beneath the stars, but all the while that my mind drifts, and I think of past travels, and of all my brothers and sisters, a part of myself pays attention to the time, and watches every bit of time slide by.

For I am not just guiding my little proa and my six brothers, I am carrying my whole village in the proa, our home island is the proa which I am guiding on a long travel, and it seems odd to me that my brothers and sisters are planting rice, are climbing up the tall trees for coconuts, are butchering a pig, are lighting cook fires on the proa, while I must sit at the stern and guide it, and pay attention to the time. My wife comes to me and pulls on my hand, and smiles, and says let us go make love, but I shrug her hand off, and tell her I must keep track of the time, and guide the rudder. My brothers are gathering to drink banana beer, and I wish I could join them, but I must hold the tiller. It is sad to be alone, and responsible, while the others are so care-free, but there is pride in it too, and I expand my chest pleasantly.

My wife pulls at my arm again, and I am almost irritated. She always wants to make love, she will never leave me alone. I turn almost with anger to tell her to stop shaking my arm, and then I am awake.

"Do you sleep, Brother?"

It is my brother shaking my arm.

"Of course I do not sleep. I was thinking deeply about the old days, and remembering many good travels."

Although I see the waves are going the wrong way in relation to the proa, I hold the rudder steady, as though I meant to go that way, and when my brother goes back to sleep, I turn back across the waves.

The sky is completely wrong. It makes me dizzy to look at it. Did a little time go, or much time? It must be only a little time. I guess an amount of time that must have gone. Then I look at the stars, thinking that that amount of time must have gone, and the stars look right again, and I continue from there. I am shaking all over, which must be from fear, because my body feels so hot I feel I am sitting too close to the fire. I rinse sea water over my head and chest, but it dries at once and the salt itches on my skin.

I keep shaking in little shudders, or convulsions, and coughing, and I see in the starlight the others are shaking too, but in their sleep. If I am wrong only a little bit about the time, then we will be heading a little bit in the wrong direction. In two days a little bit wrong will be a big amount wrong, and we will be in the great sea.

I do not sleep again, for I am very worried. My brothers are coughing and moaning in their sleep. I am terribly thirsty, but I do not dare drink, for we have already drunk too much water, and if we miss Kiri-ritti, we will perhaps need water for several days. But my brothers keep getting up and drinking, and I cannot admonish them, for if we miss Kiri-ritti, it is not their fault, it is my fault.

The sky lightens, and the sun is born, but is seems to me it happens too soon, so perhaps I slept for a greater time than I thought. So I change the rudder to where it should be if I had slept for a longer time. And then I think: how long did I go wrong to the waves, and I guess a time that I went wrong to the waves, and change the rudder to correct for that. I cannot stop myself, and take a very small drink, but it dries up in my mouth before I can swallow it.

We try to eat a little more dog-fish, but our stomach pushes it back out. We are very weak, and my brothers try not to drink water, but finally they must, and they drink as little as they can. I drink an even smaller amount. In the middle of the day, I begin thinking that maybe the sun was born at the right time, rather than too soon, so I correct back again. But then I think, in that case we have been going wrong for half the day, so I estimate, and try to correct for that.

The sun dies and I keep having terrible dreams that our island is the proa, and I am not sure if I am guiding it right. There is no rain, and the rice shoots shrivel in the ground, and the breadfruit does not come, and the coconuts have no fruit, and by accident we have given away all our pigs. But all the time I am dreaming, I keep my eyes open, and keep track of the time. I have often done that on past travels.

In the morning, our water is all used up, and we must wait until later afternoon before we reach Kiri-ritti. The inside of my mouth and my throat is like the coals we roast the pigs on. When I cough I taste blood in my mouth, and eagerly drink my blood because it is wet anyway. One of my brothers is gray and still lying on the floor of the boat. We do not look at him or say anything about him.

In the middle of the day suddenly one of my brothers sweeps the bowl through the sea-water, and fills it, and puts it to his lips.

"If you drink that, Brother," I say, "you will die."

"My thirst means more than my life," he says, and he drinks it, gulping it eagerly, it spilling over the sides of his mouth. Suddenly the others are dipping and drinking, gulping, drinking again, gagging, then sitting and looking at each other hopelessly.

We are all very weak, and only stare at one another. I keep track of the time, and hold the proa the right way to the waves.

Then one of my brothers starts up, and there is madness in his eye, and he waves his arms, and screams and gasps, and foams at the mouth, and throws himself over the side. The others are screaming, and beating their chests, and thrashing blindly, almost upsetting the proa, and one by one they throw themselves over the side, until I am alone, except for my one brother, lying gray and still in the bottom, who never woke up.

I keep track of the time, and hold the proa the right way to the waves. The coconut trees are shriveling, and drooping over the ground. The pigs are dead and rotting on the ground, flies are crawling over everything, and I have somehow steered the island to a place where the rains never come.

* * *

They sat opposite each other at the breakfast table.

"I felt sick all night," she said. "I don't think I slept for more than an hour. I think I might have fainted once. You don't know what it's like. *Oh God* I wish you could be sick like that for just one night, so you'd know what it feels like." She'd got up twice in the early morning, and made—he felt—as much noise in the bathroom as she could, to make sure he would hear it. She moved her chair back from the table and looked at her untouched breakfast.

"Everything I smell makes me sick. What's going to happen if I can't eat?" She was close to tears.

He kept looking out the window and avoiding looking at her. He wanted to say, If you just try for once to take it in stride, if you just try to grow up a little bit, and stop expecting to be babied, you would find out very quickly that it wouldn't be half as bad. You make it worse on yourself by being such a baby. I get sick like everyone else, I have days I don't feel so hot, but I don't show it, I ignore it, and the result is, it doesn't bother me so much. In our family we never showed things, we were just a bit more stoic, we would never dream of seeing a doctor short of needing major surgery. You have this thing where the least little thing that happens, you want to see a doctor, you want to have something prescribed, you want to take something, you want everybody to know about it, to feel sorry.

She was crying now. "I know you don't believe me," she was saying, and came over for him to comfort her, but he held her very coldly. He tried his best to pat her on the back and say something comforting, but he couldn't, so he finally said, "I have to go in and take that exam."

He drove out through the flats, watching to see if there were any falcons around, or if any snowy owls had shown up, but he was thinking, I don't know how much longer I can take this. He was the one, after all, who had to take all the strain of not having a job, who had to keep writing the hopeless letters of application, and get the rejections, who had to watch their savings slowly diminish no matter how little they spent, and now at home there was practically a pesthouse. At just the moment he most needed comforting himself, he got nothing but a long woeful recounting of sickness and misery. He needed to have *something* brighter in his life. What was the point of anything? Everything was dying somehow, life, love—the words of a song kept going through his head.

I don't know where we went wrong
but the feeling's gone
and I just can't get it back

For the first time ever it occurred to him that maybe one day he could possibly be unfaithful to his wife. He was still relatively young, he couldn't go on the rest of his life in dreariness.

The car was missing badly, and he knew the points needed replacing and probably it needed new valves, and fortunately driving wasn't very complicated out on the country roads, because the brakes had been nonexistent for months. Dying, everything was getting old and dying. The praying mantis they had hatched out in the spring and kept going, starting with tiny flies, then working up to house flies, and finally huge grasshoppers, as it grew in size and aggressiveness, had lost one leg, and most of one antenna, and the tips of several other legs, and injured its eye, and had now almost completed its season. They had been feeding it meat off a tweezers, but in the last couple of days it had lost all its strength, and was moping around the bottom of its jar. He remembered another symbol of death he had always wanted to work into a short story sometime: when they lived in the midwest when he was doing his degree, in the summer the fields had been filled with huge bright yellow spiders, sitting in the center of their big orb webs, and they were almost symbols of the summer itself, so big and bright, but there were fewer and fewer as the season progressed into autumn, and finally there was only a single one left, in a damaged and incomplete web in a bush right next to their front door. The orb had only about half a dozen spokes left in it, and the spider in the center had lost all but three legs, one on one side, two on the other. He read somewhere, with a feeling of sadness, that a spider is born with only a finite amount of web to spin, and when that is gone, it dies. It was almost like a classical Greek sense of fate. He saw this spider getting thinner by the day, its body shrunken and wrinkled. Although it was getting quite cold by then, he searched all over and finally found a fly, and crippled it a bit so it wouldn't struggle too energetically, and dropped it into the spider's web.

It fell right out. What little web that was left had lost its stickiness.

He tried several times to stick the fly in the web, but without success, and finally lost the fly in the tall grass.

The next day he located another fly and brought it around. The spider seemed to have no substance at all inside its shriveled abdomen. He put the fly in a tweezers, and held it directly to the spider's mouth. This was taking a chance, because the spider might panic and drop to the ground, and then it would never get back to its web again.

But he needn't have worried. The spider gratefully received the fly, instantly locking on to it with its chelicerae, and began eating it at once.

For the next several days he spent every spare minute searching for flies. He usually got them in the morning, basking on sunny walls of houses, and each day he had at least one for the spider, and watched the bag of its abdomen slowly fill out until it lost its wrinkles and fully inflated again, though a dull brown now, instead of the bright yellow of summer.

And then one night six inches of snow fell, and when he came out in the morning the web was gone without a trace.

Everything is irreversible, birth and copulation and death, eat and excrete, all down hill, the mantis dying, the car dying. He was dying. He broke his leg skiing when he was a kid, and they fixed the broken bone but ignored the snapped ligaments and torn cartilage, so that now nothing holds his knee together except the muscles around it. As long as he walked a lot and kept the muscles strong he was all right, but if he went even a short time without walking, his knee was swollen and sore, and he couldn't bend it or sit with his legs crossed. Walking, he thought with bitterness, is the main thing I do, the greatest pleasure I have, and by the time I'm old and retired and can walk as much as I want, I'll be a fucking cripple. And then, he thought, there are my marvelous teeth, full of pyorrhea and rotting away at the gums, and of course I'm doing nothing about it, and ultimately they'll all fall out, and I'll have a lovely pair of pink and white plastic choppers in a glass every night.

He had been thinking to himself lately—and this was certainly something he had never thought before—he had been thinking, if something happened to me, an accident, a plane crash, a terminal disease, maybe in some ways it wouldn't matter all that much. There are any number of problems it would solve. Although it was costing them a fortune, he had kept up his life and health insurance from when he had a job.

Just before he drove into Mt. Pleasant he passed a field which always had a very handsome bay mare in it. She had just that moment foaled (which shows how observant I am, he thought, I hadn't even realized she was pregnant), and the baby was lying black and wet at her feet, and she was licking it.

The day was tedious and boring. He rather enjoyed going to the unemployment office down in the valley near where they lived, because the lines were full of hippy kids who obviously were very satisfied with their lives and with the marvelous bounty that their weekly unemployment check meant to them. Their only fear was that they might find a job. But here in town there were fewer young people, and more desperate older women whose husbands were too sick to work, and who were looking for anything however menial, and grim resigned blacks who knew there was no possibility of their ever finding anything. He spent hours waiting around in the dreary building before he had finally taken all parts of the civil service exam. The idea was that he might get some substitute work at the post office, which, along with occasionally subbing at the high school, and J's paintings, might keep them going after the unemployment checks ran out.

He tried to tell himself that this had happened before, and he had got over it. She was just raised, as a kid, to make a big thing out of being sick, and she was over-comforted, and got lots of attention, and in his family it was simply the opposite, they ignored sickness, and so she got a bit hysterical with sickness, and in his way he did too, he would get unreasonably, inordinately angry with her, it was in a way a failing in her, but just as much one in him, and he felt guilty for being so cold to her, and thought he would make an effort to be more understanding, only he would have to be careful what he said, or else she would suddenly become a great martyr, pulling herself up from death's door to heroically serve him dinner, her face set bravely, though collapse was imminent—but he was getting angry again. He knew what she wanted was for him to ask her how she feels— which he had very carefully refrained from doing, because he knew she would tell him at length. But why couldn't he just admit her weakness, and listen sympathetically? Where was the harm to him, for Christ's sake? And he began remembering all the good things, and all the times when he had done wrong, or panicked, or made mistakes, and she had silently forgiven him, because they were both human.

When he got home, J met him at the door. "How're you feeling?" he said.

"Much better now," she said, and kissed him.

"What's the good smell?" he said.

"A new recipe for stew. I think it's come out pretty nice."

"Do you know that bay horse, just before you get into town?"

"The pregnant one?"

"Yes, actually. Anyway, she had her foal this morning, just before I came by. It was still wet. And it's amazing, when I came by this afternoon—you know, it's only *existed* for a few hours—it was standing up, wide-eyed and alert, and the sun was finally out, and it was staring with *astonishment* at a tree. Think of it."

"Speaking of new life," J said, "look at my tit."

She whipped out one breast—and her breasts had grown full and very beautiful—and wrinkling up her face to look directly down at it, she squeezed it with her fingers at the base of the nipple, and a little clear droplet suddenly appeared. "It's just colostrum," she said. He took it on his finger tip and licked it, and then he put his hand on that nice breast, and kissed her.

"Do you like me?" she said.

"Yep."

"Are you going to be good to me, and patient with me?"

"Yep."

"Do you know what?" she said, suddenly standing back and looking at him quizzically. "You ought to be punched up sometimes."

* * *

[There are some other South Seas fragments I don't know what to do with, maybe put in an appendix at the end or something, but the next connected journal entry (by Davie) I have is from back on our side of the Pacific again, in what must be the west coast of what is now Mexico, and then was still New Spain.]

We follow'd the *Coast* for severall Dayes, running short of Fresh Victual & Water, but wt no where a *Place* to put in. High *Mountaynes* came down right to the *Coast*, cover'd wt thick Forrest of *Palmas* & other Trees, lost in Clowds in the Heights, & terminating, abowte 100 ft above the *Sea*, in sheer & unscallable Rock *Clifts*, wich droppt precipitously to the daungerously crashing Surf belowe.

At length, the *Coast* began trending in-wards, & we hop'd we was intring the wide Mowthe of an open *Baye*. Indeed the Seas were less high, the water more proteckid, & *sea-Birds*, wich had been all but absent, became more numberous, partickularly a large dark *Gull*, like the *Grate Black-backt* of home [this would be the Western Gull, *Larus occidentalis*], & many *Shags* & *Pelicums* & the dark *Gannets* or *Bo-bo*'s we had seen at the *Gallapago*'s.

There was Sea Weed floating in the Water, & more sign of

[70]

Shark Finns, & sholes of *Fish* rising. We put over Trolling lines & at once beginn catching fine *Tunny Fish* the length of a *Mans* Arme. This was very good Newes indeed, for we had been on Hard *Tack* & dri'd *Bisketts* for three Months together. The Water turn'd from deep Blew to pale Green, as we approcht a sub-merg'd *Island*, & here we hove to, & put out the *Long Boat* & the *Pinace*, & took big *Groper Fish* from the Rocks so fast as we cou'd hale em in. All abowte us on the surface was big Sea *Turtles* coupling, the *Males* so intent upon theire Busyness that we easily gaff'd em aboard, but the *Fee-males*, as if less in love wt the Vice, keeping more theire witts abowte em, escap't by quickly diving. We soon learn'd to take the *Feemale*, who lay below the *Male* in the Water, 1st, & then generally we had time to take the fuddl'd *Male* as well. We sett our Anchors & spent the rest of the Daye & night in feasting wich wou'd have done a *Roman Emperour* proud, braking out some *Sack* we had long hoarded, & eating the delitious fresh *Fish*, & the *Turtle*, wich eat like very fine graned *Beef-Steak*, & we eat the *Egs* wich we cut out of the Bellies of the *Fee-males*, abowte the bigness of an Henns *Eg*, but perfectly Round, & solidly of *Yoak*, wt no white, & so rich, the 1st was a deleight to eat, the 2d neer a surfeit, & the 3d so jaded us we cou'd scarce finish it.

We spent all of the next Daye loding up wt more *Gropers* & fine big *Snappers* the length of a *Mans* Body, & a small, very Fatt *Fish*, call'd by the Spaniards, *Caballitos*, & perhaps 50 more *Turtles*, most of wich we clean'd & split & hung upon the Yards, in the *Indian* fashion, to dry in the Sunn wich show'd even & Hott in the blew Sky, wt a Fresh Brease making for perfeck drying weather. We continu'd along this wide *Baye* in mighty pleasant Spirits, & at length, when we had alreddi all but passt it, spotted the inlet to a small *Cove*, & instantly came abowte, & inter'd into it, & found a well nigh perfeck Harbourage, an immaculate Round *Baye* shelter'd by headlands on two sides, of abowte 1 *League* acrost & a bitt more in length [a league at this time was probably about three miles], & terminating in a Sandy

[71]

Beech at the end, wt a low River *Valley* beyond, giving us shelter, access to the Land, & fresh Water. Abowte half-way along, we saw *Canoas* anchor'd near the *Shoar*, where a kind of *Creek* trickl'd into the *Baye*, & peering into the *Forrest* as we passt, we spotted 2 or 3 *Huts* of *Palma*-Thatch.

We anchor'd abowte ½ Mile from the *Beech*, & paus'd to think in what attitude we shou'd present ourselfs to the *Natives*, whether they was hostile or Frendly. They soon put this out of dou't, for 3 or 4 *Indians* came riding up on *Horses* & *Mules*, (meaning they had had commerce wt the *Spanish*, & so was not intirely Wild) & wav'd to us in what appar'd a frendly manner of Greeting. In the Mean while, others had swam out to the *Canoas*, & swiftlie paddl'd em over to us. None carri'd Weapons, & all was smiling. We fill'd the *Long Bote* wt *Mirrours* & hand *Ax*'s, & such bawbles, as we thou't wou'd please em, & put into *Shoar*, where by now perhaps 50 had come o' Foot to joyne the greeting Party.

[Apparently this account is written "to the moment," for here he breaks off, and does not pick up the account for several days.]

The *Shipp* by this tyme was heavie & slowe wt *Grass* & *Barnacles*, & the *Beech* was perfeck to hale her out & give her a full careening. This meant a stay of several Dayes in this lovelie Place, wich was very agreeable to Dr *Harris*, & myself, for it gave us not onelie a chaunce to study the *Indians* & theire manner of living, but also to take some plesaunt Rambles inland to study the natural Producktions so abundant here. Lett me now in summary fashion describe the people, theire life & Customs, the *Terreyne*, it's natural Producktions.

The *Spaniards* knew of this *Baye*, & sometimes stoppt here for shelter & water & careening, & so the *Indians* had had some commerce wt em & in consequence, at least 2 of em knew enough *Espagnole* that we cou'd converse wt em, & ther bye lern a good deal abowte how they liv'd. Theire Life indeed in this sunny &

[72]

pleasaunt *Paradise* was so cloase to our 1st *Parents* lives as cou'd well be, & Dr. *Harris*, at the outsett at least, made much of theire natural goodness & simplicitie, butt I think as we came to kno' more of them, he beginn to mend his Vuws some what.

The *Area* itself was neer perfeck in convenience & natural bewtie, except that, perhaps from sheer surfeit of perfecktion, it bred in us, & in the *Indians* no dou't, an indolence we wou'd find shamefull in our northerly *Homes*. As everywhere in the areas within the *Tropicks*, day length did not alter wt the Season, but was uniformelie divided wt the Night, an equal 12 Howres of Day, & 12 Howres of Night, the sun Rising abowte 8 a Clock of the morning, & setting abowte 8 a Clock of the Evening. In all our long months of travell in these *Latitudes*, we had found no difficulty in sleeping thro' the full 12 Howres of darkness, & indeed, in the hotter months, were none averse to a midday Napp as well! I am sure this manner of carrying on will come as a Shock & Scandal to our *Countrymen* at Home in our sadly misnomer'd "temperete" *Climate*, where all is hard & energetick work all the howres of the Daye (meerly, it seems to me now, to preserve the *Body* agaynst freazing!). The tyme of Yeer now (mid Summer by *European* reckning,) was neer to the end of the dry Season, wich had run all thro' a warm, clowdless, sunny *Winter* (as badly misnam'd here as summer is wt us in *England*!). The Clowds was gathring, the temperature going up, & the *rains* preparing.

To beginn wt the *Setting*: imagine a perfeckly form'd Oval *Baye*, the Water of a breath-taking clairty, & fill'd wt Fishes of every discription, *Snappers* & heavie *Gropers* in the depths, or the interstities of Rocks, banded or spottid *Eals*, grate *Manta Rayes*; at the Tyme we arriv'd, small *Sardinas*, or *Anchovies*, was running in such numbers they fill'd the Water, & was flung out upon the *Beech* wt each braking Wave. *Tunny* of a wate of 20 lb swam in sholes, gape-mowth'd, glutting on the *Sardinas*, & so intent upon this they came blindly into shallow Water, where, once, standing on a rocky *Promentory* out from the Edg, I acktually stoopt, & siez'd one by the *Tayle* (the right-angle Finns of the *Tayle* serving

[73]

as a Handle!), & pull'd it out of the Water, & eat my Prise for Supper! But to continue: a perfeck Oval *Baye*, conneckting wt the larger *Baye* by a narrow Mowth running between 2 *Head* Lands. On either Side of the *Baye*, forested Mountaynes rising straight up into the Clowdes, at the far end, a long Sandy white *Strand*, & beyond that a River *Valley*. As was explayn'd to me, the River came steeply & rapidly down to the *Baye*, carrying Sand & Gravel befor it, especially during the *Rains*, when it rusht quite frantically. These Sands & Gravels eventually made this long line of high beech which, acting as a *Dyke*, eventually clos'd of[f] the mowthe of the *River*, wich all backt up behind in a wide shallow freshwater *Lagoon*. Since the mowth clos'd off towards the end of the Rainy Season, the *Laguna* fill'd up but slowlie after that, became stagnant, & fill'd up wt a lush growth of aquatick *Weeds*. At the moment we arriv'd, it was fill'd quite high, & we was told, tho' we did not stay to see it, that shortlie after the *Rains* (the *Aguas*) commenc't it wou'd grow so high & heavy, that it's wate caus'd it to breech thro' the *Beech* all of a sudden, scattring the Sands, & pouring out into the *Baye*, carrying all its Silt & weeds wt it. The *Baye* wou'd be muddi'd for some Dayes, & the abundance of *Weed*, dying in the Salt Water, wou'd Rot, attrackting even more tremendous sholes of small fishes & other Creatures to feed on it; & this at last attrackting grate *Sharks* & *Barracudies*, wich wou'd lie of shoare & make the *Indians* fearfull to swim in the *Baye*, whilst they was at theire heighth. In a few Weeks this wou'd be gone, the Water wou'd cleer, the *Beech* wou'd repair itself from new Sand brou't down, & the *Laguna* wou'd beginn filling agen, to repeat the Cycle the following Yeer.

For this reason there was no *Dwelling* on the Sandy *Beech*, wich else lookt so suitable & convenient. Instedd, the *Indians* liv'd along the steep Mountayneside on the Side of the *Baye*, where we had seen theire *Canoas* anchor'd when we 1st inter'd the *Baye*. They had settl'd upon a place where a stream pour'd down the Mountayne, giving em convenient Fresh water for drinking & bathing. The Water droppt in a steep *Cascada* of perhaps 200 ft, then came out to a slightlie leveller descent, & in this flatter area, hidden almost invisibly in amongst the *Co-Co* & *Coquito* & *Banano Palms*, along either side of the Stream, was dozaynes of theire *Howses*, made of *Wattle* & rooft wt *Palma* Thatch. They had dirt floors & openings for windows & doors, wt no way of closing these, & no need in the perfeck Climate. Because it was on a high Slope, the Setting was wonderfully salubrious, an almost steddy pleasaunt Brease coming in of[f] the Water kept the Ayr cool & almost completely free from *Musketos* & other Pests.

The people, we found, however, liv'd in the *Village* onelie during the dry Season. Once the *Rains*, & therefore, the Growing Season commenc't, they generally mov'd out to theire individual *Ranchos* wich they had spredd thro' out the High Lands, where they had perhaps a few *Cattel* & *Horses*, & grew the Indian *Corn*, & the *frijoles*, wich was a stapel of theire dyet.

Whylst we was ashoare, Dr *Harris*, & I, rather than living on the *Shipp*, was lett 1 of the small Howses, where we slep on hanging *Hammockas*, wich affordid us much difficultie to lern to ballance in, but wich after a few Dayes we soon came to prefer to our own Bedds for cool, Restfull Sleep in a *Tropickal* Clime. In the heat of Midday, we regularly lay in our *Hammockas* to chat, or write up our Observations, & we scarce needed to go outside to observe the Natural Producktions of the *Region*, for they was quite willing to come to us! *Lizzards* of all discriptions climb'd abowte on the Walls catching *Flies*, *Snakes* wander'd in Prospeckting for *Rats* & *Mice*, & once, wt a rumbel & shudder, the very ground beneath my Feet fell away, & an astonishing little animal the size of a *Terrier* inter'd. He had a Head I can onelie describe as like a *Griffins*, long Nose & floppy *Donkie* Ears, & a back cover'd wt Armour-like Plates, & funny scratchy little Bird-like Feet. His organs of *Sight* was but Rudimentary, & he snuffl'd wt his Nose, & lookt around bleary-Ey'd, like *My Lady* 1st thing in the Morning after an over-long Night of *Ombre*. Dr *Harris*, & I cou'd not contayne ourselfs from busting into Laughter, at wich the Creatur swiftlie exited. [He is of course describing an armadillo.]

After we had been ther but a Daye or 2, word came to us that the *Congrejos* had arriv'd, wch prov'd to be a kind of Land *Crabs*, wich appar'd regularly each Yeer as a precursor to the Arrival of the *Rains*. Suddenly they was everywhere, a fat stocky *Crab* abowte 4 inches acrost. They fedd on the dry *Palm* Thatch of the Roofs, wich seem'd to me the least nourishing Substance imaginable. But because of this prediliction of theire Dyet, they was thick abowte the *Howses*, & we soon grew accustom'd to the little snapping Clicking sound of theire eating. What we never quite got us'd to, was the fact that the *Piggs* wich run Loose thro' all the *Village* (keeping it, I must say, clean of any refuse or nastiness), deleighted in eating the *Crabs*, & at any Howre of the Daye or Night we wou'd hear the sickning *Cruntch* of them biting into 1 of these *Creaturs*.

Finest of all, was last thing of an Evning, Dr *Harris*, & I, wou'd wend our way up the Trayle thro' the *Village*, to the large *Pond* at the Top, at the base of the high *Cascade*, & ther take our liesurely *Bath* in the warm clear Water. Whylst we floted on our *Backs*, we watcht Jewel- like *Humming Birds* coming, & drinking & bathing in the spray of the Water Fall, & huge arboreal *Lizzards* lep from Branch to Branch of *Trees*, or scal'd along the clift Edg's, fighting & flaring theire Crests at 1 tother.

And agen, in the Mornings, when we have not a long Walk forward, we often amus'd ourselfs by walking into the agreably warm Water of the *Baye*, at the bottom of the *Creek* where the *Indians* anchor'd theire *Canoas*, & swimming far out into the *Baye*, arcing around to come out at length, on the white sandy *Strand*, the whole circuit perhaps 1 mile, in Water so calm & boyant we cou'd neer fall asleep in 't. I was alwayes struck, at these Times, observing the Surroundings from the Center of the *Baye*, at the seemly & perfeck configuration of the *Scene*, wich no *Artists* Pallate cou'd capture, the trees spac't, not uniformlie, but somehow wt perfeck intervals, marching stately up the steep

slopes into the misty clowdes, the Blews of the Water, the var-
igated Green of the *Forrest*, the white of the *Beech*, all beyond
discription.

But most Dayes we was to jealous of our Tyme to laze abowte.
At our 1st Chaunce, we took Provisions, colleckting *Guns*, &
hir'd 2 *Indians* for *Guides*, & to carry the Speciments we collecktid, & follow'd a Trayle, leading up thro' the *Village*, wind-
ing around to the Right of the Water Fall, & leading, ultimately,
we was assur'd, to another *Village* in the High Lands, abt a Days
Journy.

We took severall small *Birds*, some *Paroquets*, a large fowel,
call'd, after its own Voyce, *Chalacka*, a kind of *Jay* wich was all
Blew, save a black Hood over it's Head, like a Royal
Executioner, & some Gorgeous bright long-tayled *Parrots*, or
Makaws, wich the *Indians* call'd *Guacamaya*; also severall kinds
of *Ants* & *Termites* wch lookt new to us, & what lookt like a kind
of *Ottor*, tho' there was no Water Abowte. But what was most of
intrest to us was the rapid changes in *Terrayne* as we climb'd. The
Path went up by Switch-Backs, almost so steeply as we was able
to manage, wt much loss of Breath. It was at 1st thro' a *Forrest* of
Palmas; tall stately Tronks, letting in littel Light from above, so
that little grew on the Ground, & the Terreyne was rather open &
Park-like, tho' difficult to make Waye in, because of the depth of
rotting Litter. Also, any bit of *Vegetation* we toucht, & tiny *Ticks*
shower'd upon our *Bodies*, & we needed to stop & pick em off
each Other like *Monkies*. But after abowte 1000 or 2000 Feet of
Climbing, we suddenly inter'd the Clowdes, & everything
Alter'd. We was as in a shifting Mist, for all the World as if in
some Level of the *Inferno*, Trees twisting & grotesque & cover'd
over wt Thornes, writhing as tho' they cou'd contayne the Tor-
tur'd Bodies of *Suicides*, whylst down the Gloomy Corridors of
the open Path flutter'd giant white *Butterflies* like the wandring
Souls of the miserable *Dead*. And as if we was indeed abowte to
inter *Dantes Inferno*, the Path brancht off, & ther indeed stood a
stout *Leopard* [this would of course be a jaguar], like the *Sin* of

Greed or Lust, blocking our direck Waye to the *Promis'd Land*! We was to[o] Spell bound to think of firing at him, & was indeed loded wt fine dust shott for *Birds* at any Rate, but we felt no Fear looking at this grate Handsom *Beest*, wich for his Part regarded us wt the apparence of grate Intelligence & curiosity, befor slowlie, &noblie, turning, & walking of from us, not as tho' fleeing, but meerly continuing on abowte the busyness that stopping to contemplate us a moment had interruptid.

We now quicklie rose out above the Clowdes, into open sunshine, in a more temperate apparing *Woods*, tho' still unimaginably lush & vari'd by our *European* Standards, for instead of an intire *Woods* made up of some 2 or 3 kinds of *Trees*, as wt us; here there seem'd almost no 2 *Trees* alike.

Beyond us, (tho' here we turn'd back, so as not to be benighted,) the Mountaynes rose agen, into what lookt to be *Coniferous* Forrest, & so in very littel space, we had risen from lowlands *Forrest*, thro' a special *Woods* growing alwayes in Clowds, to upland *Woods*, &, had we continu'd, soon into dense *Conifers*, 4 severall Kinds of *Vegetation*, each, wt it's own peculiar Natural Producktions, for as the *Plants* & *Trees* vari'd, so also vari'd the *Birds*, the *Insecks*, &c, & this all determin'd by the heighth above Sea-Level.

Somewhat shou'd be said abowte the *Indians* themselvs. These was a dark olivey-Brown in Colour, wt straight, & sometimes bushy Black *Hair*. The *Men* was sturdily built, & very handsom in theire Physiognomies. Indeed the Childern, *Boyes* & *Girls*, was extremelie Bewtifull, wt fine bright Smyles that seem'd to make the Sun shine the brighter when they came out. The *Men* seem'd onelie to grow the handsomer as they grew older, but the yong *Girls*, who bath'd in the Rivers unasham'd befor us, & was so lovely to behold that we had to tear ourselfs awaye from the sight of em, had even from the start something thick & square in theire Shapes, for they had no *Waists*, their broad short *Torsos* falling straight down to theire *Hipps*, & this tendencie increasing

[78]

wt Age, they shortly grew Thick, then Fatt, & lost theire good looks. But at 14 or 15 yeers, these yong *Naiads* of the River cou'd destroy the sleep of at least 1 sobersides old Natural Philosopher—luckilie they was perfeckly Chaste, else ther might have been serious Trouble betwixt these proud *Indians* & our *Saylors*.

The *Village* at wich we stay'd was 1 of 5 *Villages* in an Area extending 10 Myles along the *Coast*, & some 30 Myles Inland, connecktid by a system of Trayles, all comprising a single *Communidad*, or Communitie, rul'd over by a body of *Elders*, who judg'd Disputes & such, tho' in general the *People* was left pretty much to theire own Devices, & it seem'd that meer pressure to be acceptid by the community at large was sufficient to make each 1 Law-Abiding. Just befor we came, a *Man* had run Crazy & murther'd his *Wife*. Ther was of course no System of Prison or Execution, & what the *Elders*, after much deliberation finally decided, was to go in a Body & tell this *Man* that he cou'd no longer reside in the Communitie. This Punishment, seeming so laughably Mild to us, was in Fact, to these *People*, the cruellest Imaginable, & the *Man*, tho' let to live in some other nearbye Communitie, was pining awaye, so that meer Social Pressure, as I say, is evidently enough to make of these *People* good *Citizens*.

Another part of theire Oeconomie is instructive: As the *People* are neerlie self-sufficient unto such items as Food, & Shelter, it is possible that a system of Barter wou'd ne'er have become pronounc't in em. However, the *Spaniards* coming, & having need of Provision from em, & imploying theire Labour to help Beech & Careen theire *Shipps*, institutid the Custom of Paying em wt Cash. This was like adding to *Paradise* the *Forbidden Tree*, for it brou't out Aspeckts of the *People* wich else might never have been Seen. We saw this, 1st of all in that the *Indians*, whylst they acceptid from us *Ax*'s & *Mirrours* & such as *Gifts*, wou'd not take them in exchaunge for Labour or Goods, but insistid on *Coin* of the *Realm*, wich they was obviously Mad to get theire Hands on. It was little enough they askt for, & this we readily compli'd wt.

What was of intrest to me was to observe theire use of it once they had it, for they knew not what to do wt it. For the most, 't was an imbarrassment & an incumberance to be ridd of so quicklie as Possible, before theire *Hands* was scortcht by the meer holding of it. Nothing was more comickal, & at the same Time Melancholly, then to see an other-wise Sane & Sober *Man* recieve his *Wage* of us, & immediately beginn looking for a Waye to spend it. This was most readily compasst by going to a sort of *Public Howse* maytayn'd by 1 of the *Indians* down on the *Beech*, where a sort of Spiritous *Liquor* was prepar'd from the fermentation of the pulpy & gelatinous *Foliage* of a kind of flowring Tree grown here for that Purpose [*Maguey*, probably, an Agave from which Tequila is still made]. The poor *Indian*, wt his *Coppers* clutcht in his *Hand*, devoted the Daye to drinking, wt little Evident injoyment, intill such time as his *Money* was expendid. To help get this over wt, he invited all of his Frends & passersbye to drink a *Tost* wt him, & all were in duty bound to Comply, even myself when I mistakenly chaunc't by, tho' I personally found it a most Poysonous libation, the least Swallow of wich gave me Indigestion. His money at last gone, the miserable *Creetur*, weeping & sobbing, wretching out his *Guts*, weaving dronkinly, found his Waye home to his grimly waiting *Wife* & frighted *Childern*.

But, you may wonder, at the *Proprietor* of the little *Taverna*. Here is a *Beeing* of another Stamp intirely, tho' presumably bred & born into the identickal *Society* wt the Rest. But here is a *Man* as knowlidgible of accompts, credits, debits, (tho' illiterate, wt out the least Notion of *Maths*. besides simple Addition!) as the meenest Money-Lending *Jew*. Wt none of the others Itch to be Rid of his shekels, he had the contrary Itch to amass em all unto himself, & in such an innocent *Society*, he had little difficulty in this, for he devoted himself to the easing of his *Neigbors* of theirs, & indeed lookt at every *Humane* transacktion as another Waye to inrich himself. It was he, for instance, who Lett us our *Lodging*, tho' we had hospitably been offer'd Lodging free in every other Place we had stoppt. It was he who maytayn'd the *Taverna*, wich not onelie profitted from his own *People*, but was, I am asham'd to say, the Scene of much dissipation from our own *Saylors* in theire tymes of Liesure. But this was onelie a beginning, for as he amass't *Cash*, he us'd it to buy Material Goods from his *Fellows*, knowing he wou'd soon enough regayne the *Money* by selling of Dross, so that where formerly the *Cattle, Horses, Mules, Jack-asses, Pigs*, was own'd neerly in Common Amongst the *Community*, now all was Own'd by him, to be Rented to those in need. When the crop of *Indian Corn* came in, & was plentifull & cheap, he bougt of it copiously, & had it stor'd in a large inclos'd *Building* of his Construction. When later in the Year *Corn* was scarce & thus deer, he now brou't it out & sold it of an inmense Profitt to his else hungry *Naybourss*.

But the very Fine & instructive *Moral* in all this is that his machinations was to no Poynt. In this lonely *Community*, lockt in by *Sea* on the 1 Hand, & Trackless houling *Wilderness* on tother, ther is no Luxury, no Opulence, on wich to spend grate Welth, ther are no fine *Stately Homes* to build, since a simple open Shack is all that is known here, & moreover suits very well wt the smileing Clime. In short, all that is Gracious & Pleasaunt & Nourishing in the *Place* is given freely of *Nature*, to the *Man* who but reeches to gather it in. So that in amassing all the local Welth, what a pitifull Mess of Pottage at last, his stincking piles of *Spanish* coppers & silver! All he has gayn'd of it, besides the dispickable pleasur of often telling it thro' his *Fingers*, is the harty & well deserv'd Hatred & disdayne of all his *Fellows*, & in this isolated *Village*, Fellowship is the onelie good of reel Valew.

[date illegible], *New Spain*, 20° 50′ N of the *Line*. Took aboard: 21 *Dear;* 44 *See Turtels;* 421 divers *Fowells;* 60 Jars Water; 51 bundles Faggots; 20 *Wild Piggs;* 2,200 *Limes;* 5 cwt *Plantaynes;* 5 cwt *Maise;* 375 *Co-Cos.*

[A very odd thing happens to me as I read this: I find myself envying Davie, envying him his bachelor freedom, the excitement and pleasure of being a naturalist in a new and fantastic place, the young girls bathing in the river, the basilisk lizards leaping overhead, the hot sun on his shoulders.

Why it's odd is because Davie is dead. He's been dead for over 200 years, in fact he dies miserably almost within that very year I am reading about. I'm alive, so even if my life were a great deal less favored and fortunate than it happens to be, it would still be preferable to being dead for 200 years, right? Okay, but what about someone who won't be born for another 200 years from now. I'm alive and he's not, so I'm more fortunate? Or is he more fortunate because after I've been cold in the grave for 200 years like Davie, he'll be out in the sunshine? Life is immortal in every moment. Because Davie happened to write down these good moments in his life (at a time when I didn't exist), and write them down very well, here they are as fresh as though he were just blotting the ink. A reader 200 or 2000 years from now looking at this book will see Davie's account and mine side by side as if taking place at the same moment, as equidistant from him as stars seem to be from earth. Let me remind you, O Future Reader, that our lives are (note the verb tense)[12] just as fortunate as yours, even though the worms have scattered our bones. Indeed my long careful study of history seems to be leading me to the conclusion that, in an important sense, there is no such thing as history. Oh, technology changes, for better or worse. No doubt I am *selectively* enjoying Davie's life: I envy him his young bathers, his exotic birds, but not the time he was losing his wife in childbirth, or the time he was dying in the arctic bleakness, and you, Future Reader, need not envy me the moment of my death, perhaps from a sickness curable in your time, but you might very well envy me the moment—a few moments from now—when my wife awakes from her nap, warm and lazy as a cat, and like a cat alertly conscious of tiny signs of life within her, and she will call me to her, and stretch, and reach up for me. As her pregnancy continues she grows daily more beautiful and desirable to me.

She is calling.][13]

[12]PRESENT TENSE!

[13]THIS VERY FUNNI HAHA JOKE ON WE   THEN/TIME MAN TALK TO WE   OK   WE   TALK   TO   NO-MORE-EXIST   THEN/TIME   MAN:

NO THEN/TIME MAN WE NO "envy" U WHEN U GO FEEL/FUK PREG "wife" THEN/TIME "wife" CARRI BABI FOR 9 MO VERI UNCOMFI VERI UGLI VERY MANI DANGER TO MUCH MORE SAFE AN COMFI TO TAKE OUT AT 3 MO WHEN TINI THEN MAKE GRO UP PERFEC IN SELLO

BUT WHAT U SAI BOUT TIME VERI INTEREST I U VERI ADVANCED - WHEN I YONG I STUDI "TIME" I STUDI "history" BECUZ MI BAG LANG/LIT I VERI INTEREST IN WORDS WORDS HAVE CHANGE VERI MUCH TAKE FOR EGSAMP THIS 2 WORDS "TIME" AN "history" THEN/TIME WORD "time" BE SOMETHING THAT MOVE FROM 1 PLACE TO NOTHER FOR EGSAMP "time is flying" "time is passing" "we are running out of time" "where did the time go?" NOW/TIME "TIME" BE MORE FIXED FOR EGSAMP WE SAI "NOW/TIME" "THEN/TIME" "SLEEP/TIME" "WAKE/TIME" WE NOW/TIME NO MORE USE WORD "history" "history" GO FROM BEGINNING/TIME UP TO END OF THEN/TIME THIS BE WHEN THINK/ TECHS LERNED EVERTHING NOW EVERTHING BE KNOWED THER BE NO MORE CHANGE ALL BE PERFEC AN THERFOR BE NO MORE "history"

BUT George Herbert (I CALL U BI NAME U HAVE VERI ADVANCED NOW/TIME NAME U NAMED FOR GREAT/TERRIF POET LIKE WE ALL BE NAMED FOR FAVE POETS OR THINK/TECHS MI NAME HAMLET-EDIPUS (SHAKE HANDS!) BUT George BECUZ MI BAG LANG/LIT I HAVE READED MANI THEN/TIME BOOKS SO MAIBI I UNDERSTAND U MORE THAN U THINK (MAIBI I JUST T I N I BIT "envy" U George WHEN U GO FEEL/FUK PREG "wife" THIS STRANGE TO THINK: BUT HOW DID "she" LOOK? HOW DID "she" FEEL? PROBLI UGLI I VERI OLD MAN AN BEGIN TO HAVE FUNI THOTS AGEN)

I TELL U TRU STORI WHEN I YONG OF CORSE I READED MANI THEN/ TIME BOOKS MOST TRU-BOOKS BUT ALSO MANI LIE-BOOKS I TO MUCH LIKED THEN/TIME LIE-BOOKS BUT THEY VERI PUZZLING THEY MAKED I THINK PUZZLING THOTS I GOED TO SOCIAL MEETS AN SHARED THAT LIE-BOOKS MAKED I FEEL THESE THOTS MI GUD FREND THERE MARX-EINSTEIN SAID TO MI THIS UR OWN BIZZ TO READ THEN/TIME LIE-BOOKS IF U LIKE E V E R - B O D I H I S O W N G U V BUT STILL WE WORRI/SWEAT FOR U THEY CAN BE TO MUCH DANGERUS (NOT TO US WE DONT MIND BUT TO U TO MAKE U UNHAPPI) DO U FEEL THEY BE DANGERUS?

I SAI YES MAIBI BECUZ THEY MAKED MI THINK: I WANT TO BE DIFF

[They were of course doing lots of transects and charting and so on as they came, and I have a few scattered pages of figures etc. in the Captain's hand, but his papers in general suffered the most depredations, and I don't know enough about the navigational parts to know what to do with what remains. At any rate, the chief design was always the seeking of that elusive northwest passage around the New World, which was itself (the New World) still only imperfectly known. Was the west coast, for instance, part of a single continent connected to the east coast, or was there water in between? At any rate, now the ship was moving up the west coast of North America, preparing for the plunge around the top. It was known that the passage, if it existed, would be locked in ice for most of the year, and the plan obviously was to work their way up to the pack ice in the spring, then simply wait around for leads to open, and if for a brief period during mid-summer the water was open, to dart through and come out to the Colonies and fame.

This next section I have (by Davie) picks them up in what can only be the interior of Puget Sound, a major discovery in its own way, since explorers for another century at least went on missing the entrance to the Sound, and kept on up the west coast of Vancouver Island. But of course since their papers were lost until now, they got no credit for it.

Here they are, anyway, going through probably the San Juan Islands, and this is tremendously interesting to me, because this is where I live, and when they come ashore, it might be on land I have walked on myself. Most immediately interesting to me, naturally, is the bird life they encountered.]

FROM EVERBODI! ALSO I THINKED (BECUZ I BE MAN W/ BABI-CARRING BODI) I THINKED MAIBI I WILL CARRI BABI 9 MO!

MARX-EINSTEIN SAI: THIS UR BIZZ U DO WHAT U THINK RIGHT - EVERBODI AT SOCIAL MEET SAI THE SAME BUT THEN THEY ASK: DO U THINK THIS IS RIGHT? DO U THINK MAIBI WHEN U A BABI UR SELLO NOT HAVE TO MUCH OXI? MAIBI U CAN HAVE BRANE SELLS FIX W/ NURO PLASTICINE? IF U THINK? IF U WANT U SAI THIS UR BIZZ

THEY AR SO VERI NICE-KIND! I GOED AN HAVED MY BRANE SELLS FIXED THEN I HAPPI AGEN (I STILL SOMETIME HAVE PUZZLING THOTS BUT THEY NO BOTHER I NOW)

[84]

I pick up this *Journal* after a hiatus of more than 2 Monthes during wich my illness & dispondencie over my miserablie infecktid *Teeth* has left me to depress'd to want to record my daylie feelings & impressions, as my Wont, since on no accn't wou'd I want ever to remind myself of these Dayes when, at its lowest Moments, I feered I cou'd not tolerate the Payne of continu'ing my *Life* another Howre. Still I attempned to make a few *Tripps* ashoare, did some colleckting, & doggidly kept up my detayl'd *Latin* notes of everie new *Creatur* observ'd. [Davie's technical scientific notes, all in Latin, make up in bulk perhaps two-thirds of the MS I have. These will all be properly taken care of, but there is no place for them here. As nearly as I can pick out the Latin, they are of fantastically precise descriptions of plumages, colors, sepals, etc., and a numbered list of all specimens taken with dates and circumstances, etc.] Two Mornings agoe, I realiz'd at Last that no Payne cou'd exceed the Payne I already suffer'd; & I allow'd Dr *Harris*, as he had been wanting to do from the Start, to excise out 2 impacktid *Molars*. The Payne was exquisite, & I bledd & swell'd for 2 Dayes; but when I wak'd this Morning I was my own *Man* agayne, & the Bliss can scarce be imagin'd, e'en by me: for I look back wt amazement at those black moments of Dispair when I consider'd taking my Life, & I think to my *Self* how often in *Life* a small Trouble inmediately befor our *Eys* blocks us from Seeing the Manifould Good of all Life abowt us.

Lett me pick up my *Narration* now, at the Termination of *Sepr*. We had been travelling for 100s of *Leagues* up a most Specktacular Coast of a Dense *Forrest* of Gigantic coniferous *Trees*, so inpenitrible we cou'd not make our Waye inland at all, except where large *Rivers* came out to the *Sea*, wich we cou'd navigate in our *Botes*. In the distance behind the Coastal *Forrests* was 1 spectackular snow-cappt *Peak* after the other, perfeck *Volcanic* cones of Prodigious Heighth, some 1 or 2 apparing to exhude Steam from *Vents* neer their Tops. Ther was never a time, all up this *Coast*, when, weather allowing, at least 1 such

Mountayne was not in vuw. But tho' we cou'd make little Waye inland, we nonetheless, once we reacht these northern *Latitutdes*, far'd well for Fresh *Victual*. Abundant Rivers & Creeks suppli'd us wt Sweet Water, & the countless Multitudes of *Water Fowell* was continually sweeping bye us in Wave after Wave, moving south befor the Expeckted *Winter*. These was mostlie *Divers* [loons, *Gavia* spp.] & black *Sea-Ducks* [he no doubt means scoters (*Melanitta* spp.), still very common], & also tremendous nos. of delitious Fatt grey *Geese* [probably Canadas].

We inter'd a long *Strait* this Morning [the Strait of Juan de Fuca, if I am correct] wich we discover'd by chaunce Yesterdaye pursuing *Water Fowel* in the *Botes*. The *Strait*, some 5 *Leagues* acrost, trended all most due E. To the S giant snowcappt *Peaks* rose direcktly up from the Sea, unimaginablie grand in the cleer Ayr. [These would be the Olympic Mountains.] The low lands on either side of us continu'd the dense, inpenitrible *Forrest*, wich stretcht in land, so far as the *Ey* cou'd see. (Mr *Mountague*, allmost cri'd, to see this *Timber* going to waste, wich cou'd build a 1,000 migtie *Fleets*.) Regularlie spac'd along the *Shoar*, in *Trees* o'er hanging the Water, was the grate bulkie Nest of *Sea Eagles*. The *Eagles* themselfs, tho' in the mayne past theire nesting Season, was abundant, sitting atop everie snagg *Tree*, or flying powerfully over our Heads. These had been common all up the *Coast*. At 1st we thou't ther was 2 severall Kinds, 1 magnificentlie plumag'd wt a dark brown, all most Black Bodie, & snowie white Head & Tayle; t'other maynelie Black, but often irregularlie mixt wt White on the Bodie, & under the Wings. But when we collecktid these, & held em in the Hand (& what magnificent *Creaturs*, full 2 *stone* in Wate, & 7 *ft* in Wing Span), we perceiv'd the black mottl'd was but the *juvenile* form of t'other. Indeed we then saw a few intermediate, still black Mottl'd on the Bodie, but beginning to form white Head & Tayle. If possible, the Waters of the *Strait* was even more densely populatid then the open Sea had been wt sholes of *Seels*, large heavie *Ottors*, *Porpoise*, & *Killers* particularlie numberus, as well as larger *Whales*. Skein after skein of Grey *Geese*, & now Snowie *Geese* & *Swanns* as well, continu'd to fill the Skie over head. The Surface of the Water was as it were Carpetid wt *Auks* in teeming 1,000s, wt many colorfull & curiously tuftid *Sea Parrots* [Tufted Puffins, *Lunda cirrhata*]. At almost everie Moment we cou'd see the flashing *Peregrine Faulcon* making his tremendous stoops to knock some hapless *Auk* or *Wader* out of the Skie. Perhaps most impressive, after the *Eagles*, was the numbrous Giant *Gulls*, black, or black & white, wt Wing Spanns all most surpassing the *Eagles*. We took some of these, & found they eat very well. [He is certainly talking about the Short-tailed Albatross, *Diomedea albatrus*, nearly extinct now, wiped out by Japanese plume hunters at the beginning of this century. Although there are only one or two Washington records for it this century, its bones commonly occur in kitchen middens of Puget Sound Indians, and many later explorers of the region commented on the commonness of these big birds.][14]

I was standing at the *Bow*, injoying the Specktacle, injoying the warm Sunny Daye, injoying my new recover'd Helth, in fact overwhelm'd wt the abundant mercies of my *Life*, as if *God* ment to repaye me for my some time unhappinesses. Dr *Harris*, was wt me, smoaking a Pipe thou'tfullie, wich is the neerest he will allow himself to confess to the feeling of Pleasur, when our Captain, Mr *Mountague*, jin'd us, wt grate excitment in his countenance.

Gentlemen, quoth he; we have now been trending neer duw East for twentie-five *Leagues*, wt no sign of a Halt, & I am convinc't we shall find none, for I verily believe we have discover'd the North-West *Passage*! I hearby name this, to the eternal glorie of his Majistie King *George* of *England, Scotland, Ire Land & Wales*: MOUNTAGUE STRAIT!

Dr *Harris*, commenc't a suddayne Coughing Fitt.

However, in 2 more Howres the many small *Isles* we had been constantlie passing, grew more & more numbrous, & beginn

[14]THESE NAMES ALL BE OF VERI RARE BUGS THAT SOON GETTED LOST IN HE'S TIME   BUT ALL NOW SAVE ON MIKE-TAPE

crowding together, intill shortlie, by Evening Fall, we found ourselfs up agaynst a solid & unyielding wall of *Land*, & made our Anchor for the *Night*.

Sep: 30—Oct: 7. We now spent severall frantick Dayes trying 1 Passage after tother, but all to no avayle, as they persistid in dead-ending. At length Mr *Mountague*, was forc't to give over his Hopes of discovering a *Passage* thro', & we beginn to think once more of working our Waye N, our Desseign being to reach the S limit of the *Pack Ice*; & ther over *Winter*, waiting for the Ice to open up in the following *Summer*.

Altho' the captayne was frustratid in his Hopes of finding an expeditious *Passage* thro' to the East, I did discover 1 peice of Information wich we all agreed was of considerable importance: On the 6th, when we putt ashoar for Water & Fire Wood, I forc'd myself in land thro' the *Forrest* wt Grate effort, & at length came to an opening, where I colleckted a large *Turdus*, or *Thrush*, very like our *Black Bird* in size & shape, & in it's call notes. 't Was an extreamlie handsom *Bird*, black on the Head wt a White Ey-Ring, slate-grey on the back & Tayle, white under-tayle Coverts, & brick Redd Breast. Why this discoverie is so significant, is that I have seen this *Bird* figur'd in a book I perus'd just befor imbarcking on this trip, "The Natural History of *Carolina*". Ther it was denominatid a *"Robin"*, (tho' it looks very little like one, & is obviously 1 more Case of the *Colonials* attempning to give familiar names to the new *Creaturs* encounter'd in this new *Land*.) My Poynt is—& when I offer'd this to Dr *Harris*, & Mr *Mountague*, they both agree'd that it was well taken—my Poynt is, that if a land bird found in *Carolina* is also fround here, then this is certaynelie a single *Continent* or Land Mass. [Catesby's *The Natural History of Carolina, Florida, and the Bahama Isles* came out a few years before the *Venture* left England. There is much of interest to the ornithologist here. First of all, it will be noticed that though they have just finished coming up the coasts of California, Oregon, and Washington, undoubtedly going ashore on several occasons, this was the first time the sharp-eyed

Davie had encountered a robin. In fact, from accounts of 19th-century naturalists, we know that until the last 100 years, the robin was a shy reclusive deep forest bird, not overabundant in numbers. It is only in recent history that the robin has quite altered its behavior, to come out and make its way with man, and, in the abundant "edge" that our building and lumbering and agriculture make, to become one of our commonest species. And note his accuracy: the European Robin (*Erithacus rubecula*), which is the robin of "who killed cock robin?" is a tiny little bird with a bright red breast. The first colonists, seeing our big lumbering migratory thrush (*Turdus migratorius*) and noticing its brick-red breast, immediately began calling it a robin, but actually it is very closely related to the European Blackbird (*Turdus merula*), a big all-black thrush identical to the American robin in habits, call notes, etc. (It is not at all related to the birds we call blackbirds.) If you sit on the edge of a lawn in Britain, for example, you will very soon see this all black robin walking along the grass pulling up worms.

Up to this time only the Atlantic and the Pacific coasts of America had been explored, and it was anyone's guess what was in between—possibly another ocean. Davie's noting that the bird he found is identical to the one found in Carolina does indeed, from an historical standpoint, constitute the first real proof that America was a continuous single continent all the way across, though this had of course been strongly suspected before.]

[This little note of Dr. Harris's belongs here, and perhaps explains what was going on in his mind when he was standing at the bow "smoaking a Pipe thou'tfullie."]

On 2 Occassions now, I have notid some Thing perhaps of interest to the *Medickal Philosopher*. On our finall long Haul passt many Barren *Isles* in the *Southern Sees*, & then making over thro' vast expansis of See to this *Coast* agayne, when wee was perforce limitid to Hard Tack & Salt *Pork & Beef*; the familiare

Signes of *Scurvie* beginn to show themselvs; onelie, as many observours have notid it befor, to Vanish as by Magic the moment wee inter'd sholing Waters in *Nueva Espagna*, & commenc't eating Fresh *Victual* agayne. It has long been suspecktid that the absence of some Item of *Dyet* is the *prima causa*. But I suspeckt now, & indeed this has also oft been suggestid in theorie, that 'tis a meer absence of *Fresh* Victual, rather then an absence of any partickular Victual. For why? Because on our long Haul N thro' the Barren & desart Lands of *Nueva Espagna* above the *Tropicks*, intill wee reecht the present smiling *Land*, wee was agayne reduc't to Salt or Dri'd *Victual*, not even stoping to Catch *Fish* in our hurry to pass thro' the dessickatid Land befor our Water was exhaustid, & yett this Tyme wt no *Scurvie*. The onelie difference betwixt this Haul, & the previous, is that during our Careening stop in *Nueva Espagna*, wee had layd Aboard many cwt. of *Limes*, wch wee all us'd for Sawse on our dri'd *Fish*, & squeazd in our Water to make it refreshing. The addition of this Fresh *fruit* to our stale Meels may well have been the soveriegn Remedie.

[Bravo, Dr. You are on the point of discovering, or at any rate demonstrating, what Captain Cook did not prove to the world for another forty years or so. Had you lived to write up your discovery, many lives might have been saved in the intervening years. In fact, by an odd confluence of time, we have three signal discoveries coming up at this moment, yours on scurvy (Cook was to use the very limes you are discussing to prevent scurvy in his sailors, and British sailors to this day are called "limeys"), Davie's proof that America is a single, continuous land mass, and Captain Montague's discovery of the entrance to Puget Sound.

Now back to Davie again.]

I pick up my *Narrative* agayne after a Gap of more then a Month. We explor'd Passayges to the S & found em all quicklie to Dead-End, & concludid we was in a deep *Baye*. We workt our Waye tediously N, Charting as we went, not kno'ing wether we must ultimately come full Circle & exit from the *Baye* by the same Channel we inter'd it, or wether ther wou'd be another Exit to the N. Indeed we all continu'd to Nourish Hopes the Passayges migt trend E agayne, & we discover the Waye acrost to the *Colonies* after all.

I say we went *Tediously*, for in spite of the o'erwhelming Bewtie of the *Vistas*, & the grate intrest of the Natural *producktions*; after the 1st 2 Dayes, when the strong on-Shoar Winds abated, we travell'd constantlie in a Clowd all most like a fine Mist of *Musketo's*, & 't is scarce conceivable the unpleasantness of these Pests incessantlie biting of us Daye upon Daye. We wore all our thickist Cloathing, & dress'd Scarfes abowte our *Faces*, & finally took to the Desprit expedient of smearing our Faces & Heads wt *Seal* Grease, wich indeed discourag'd the *Musketo's*, but made us smell so Fowel we was soon plagu'd by Swarms of *Flies*, wich climb'd down into our Cloaths, & fowelld our Food. Next, from our Careening stop in *New Spain* we had pickt up nos. of *Ratts* wich had proliferatid to an extent none cou'd remember seeing on a *Shipp* befoar, & had spoyl'd or eat quantities of our food, devouring every Thing that was not firmly secur'd, & had grown so bold & rapatious they came near to siezing the very Morsels out of our *Mowths*. Then to Capp our Miserie, a cold dreer Rayne commenc't to fall, & fell Daye upon Daye wt no surcease, till all that we own'd was Wett thro', & blown wt *Mould* & *Mildew*, & no chaunce ever to dry.[15]

And yet some moments of Bewtie I wou'd not trade even had they cost me a life-time of Miserie. One Morn when the Rain abated, Dr *Harris*, & I, went in the *Bote*, up a small River wt the *Boyes*, who had come to catch *Salmon* wich was running in such nos. they colour'd the Water Red wt theire Bodies. We had them

[15]POOR THEN/TIME MAN!   TELL ME George DO U TRULI WANT THIS TIMES BACK WHEN GERMS AN BUGS AN ANIMALS MAKE ALL UNHAPPI?   NOW NO MORE "Pests"   AN RAIN MOSTLI FALL ONLI IN AGRI QUADS

put us ashoar, & we thrust ourselvs into the neer inpenitrible *Spruce* Forrest, hanging wt *Mosses* & *Lickens*, sprouting wt bright & grotesque *Fungi*. Ther was no approaching to the acktual *Ground*, it was so o'er lay'd wt a jumble of dead Tronks & Limbs. In fact we made our onelie progress by walking along the falln Tronks, often 10 or 15 Feet above *Terra Firma*, very laborious Travell over slippery Bark, drencht wt Wet from all that we toucht, wt at 1st nothing to reward us but the distant Cronking of *Ravens*.

But then we stoppt to catch our breth, (we had onelie come at most 100 ft.,) & all at once, in the stillness, heard the most perfeck & purist Flute-like wistle. In an instant, that wistle was answer'd by another a full 2 *tones* higher, &next, from another quarter, by 1, 2 *tones* lower then the 1st, then another in some intermediate *tone*; & this amazing chorus continu'd for 2 or 3 Minutes. The singing of the *Angels*, mayhap, is much like this, I remarckt to Dr *Harris*, & he agree'd that if 't were so, he shou'd at once mend his Life. At length we spottid 1 of the *Choristers*, & in apparance he equall'd the bewtie of his Song, a large *Thrush*, very like the misnam'd American "*Robin*", but crisper & at once softer in his Plumage, blew slate on the back, russet beneath, wt a blew-grey Band acrost the Breast. [He of course is perfectly describing the song and appearance of the Varied Thrush, *Ixoreus naevius*.]

I fir'd my *peice*, & droppt him into the Chaos of Jumbl'd Tronks & Limbs, & we play'd the very *Devil* recovering him. When at length Dr *Harris*, pickt up the lovly Thing, he stroak'd back its feathers in his Hand, & said dryly: I suppose had it been an *Angel* in very Fact, we wou'd still have made it a Victim to *mans* Curiosity. Not True at all, quoth I: I was onelie charg'd wt Dust—an *Angel* wou'd have requir'd *Pellets* at the Least!

Oct: 20, 49° N of the Line. Took aboard: 60 jars of Water; 70 bundles of Faggots; 531 *Water Fowells*; 19 Dear, 4 cwt *Salmons*; 7 Barrells *Seel* Oyl

[Davie wrote "a small Trouble inmediately befor our *Eys* blocks us from seeing the Manifould Good of all Life abowt us."

I think I have somehow come through the lowest point of my absurdly fortunate life, and in retrospect, it seems to have been nothing more serious than Davie's toothache, was in fact attributable to nothing more than useless worrying over not having a job, compounded by my over-reaction to J's over-reaction to her morning sickness.[16] In fact, the sickness lasted only a week or so, and since then she has been blooming with health. And though I still don't have a job, I feel much easier about being unemployed. I passed the civil service exam with a very high score which means that at some future time I am in danger of getting a job with the post office, and suddenly thinking of how grim and confining it would be to work every day including Saturdays, with only two weeks vacation a year, has made me begin to savor my present state, for having the entire day to myself barely suffices me. Another worry that has been hanging over my head was the likelihood that the nuclear reactors in our area would go into operation, but this worry has been undercut by the absurdest of ironies: I had put on my unemployment forms in the past I had had experience working with a surveying team, and now suddenly the employment office has put me on alert that I may be employed (at some menial level) to assist a team surveying the limits of the reactor site. The idea of surveying the wild densely forested hillside back of the river valley strikes me as so pleasant (even Thoreau allowed surveying as an acceptable way of making a living) that I immediately found my politics subverted.

But another reason for my high spirits was the privilege of observing this on the way home today: J and I had gone into Mt.

[16]NOW/TIME NO MORE HAVE MORNING SICK NO MORE HAVE TOOTH "ache" (BECUZ OF TOOTH PLASTI-COTE) NO MORE HAVE "ache"! ALSO EVERBODI HAVE TO MUCH HAPPI JOB IF HE WANTS (EVERBODI WANTS)

[93]

Pleasant to do our shopping and on our way back through the flats, I suddenly tromped on the brakes, and would no doubt have dumped all our groceries to the floor if the brakes weren't so shot the best I could do is slowly decelerate and coast to a halt.

Almost overhead, an immense black Peale's falcon (the large, dark, Pacific Northwest race of the Peregrine Falcon) was balanced on a power line. We were watching with appreciation this fierce bird (the "Broad Arrow" as 18th-century British falconers used to call it, that being its shape when it made its spectacular stoops at game birds), when it suddenly flew over us at great speed, heading for a spot on the stubble field opposite us.

Just before it touched down on the ground, a female marsh hawk flew up suddenly, and we saw the peregrine had bossed the marsh hawk off some small animal it had caught and now stood on it itself. Raptors are common here in winter, and there is much piracy in their constant competition for food.

From out of nowhere, suddenly there were three, then four, and finally *nine* marsh hawks flying about the peregrine, angry as hornets. One after another, as they gained courage, they would fly at the peregrine, which, remaining sitting on the ground, at the last moment would raise its wings in threat, and the marsh hawk would veer off. Still, they were bothering it, so, carrying the prey animal in its claws, it took off and came flying towards us, all the marsh hawks after it. All at once there was a great conflation of violently flapping birds, the prey animal dropped to the ground, and when everything got sorted out, there was a handsome Rough-leg, a kind of large arctic hawk, standing proudly on the animal. The light-weight marsh hawks buzzed it for a bit, but it did not even deign to notice them.

The episode did not end there, for the peregrine, flying again over the car and heading into the field on our side of the road, no doubt in a foul mood, dropped down to buzz an innocent Red-tailed Hawk sitting on a fence post. The red tail took off with the peregrine in pursuit, but it was not so worried by the falcon that, when it spotted a mouse a moment later, it didn't hesitate to drop down and pluck it out of the field. The peregrine accelerated and now buzzed it in earnest. The hawk quickly dropped the mouse and made for the cover of some trees, and the peregrine landed to eat his hard if dishonestly earned meal.

The peregrines lose these battles as often as they win them. A month before, J and I were standing watching a peregrine sitting in the snag top of a tree about 100 feet from us. The tide was out, and he was surveying an exposed mudflat. A hundred yards from him, five or six goldeneye were dabbling about in a shallow channel of water cutting through the mud. Suddenly the peregrine launched himself and flew at them at terrific speed. If they had stayed on the water—as most ducks do when a peregrine flies overhead—they might have been all right, for peregrines generally only take flying birds. But these ducks panicked and flew for it. It was much too fast for us to see the actual strike, but suddenly the falcon went into a steep climb, and one of the ducks went bouncing end over end across the mud. The falcon was making a wide turn to come back for the bird it had struck, but an opportunistic bald eagle had snuck in behind it, and when the peregrine returned to the mud, the eagle was already eating the duck.

Well, watching all these raptors interacting had us already feeling good, and as we walked in the door of the house, the phone was ringing. It was the lady who runs the gallery in Seattle calling to say J had sold two paintings, and a check would be in the mail tomorrow.

I decided maybe I would play for the long haul after all. I phoned and got an appointment to have my car worked on, and I phoned and got an appointment to have my teeth worked on.

That night we screwed an amazing number of times for such an old man, and such an enormous wife.][17]

[17]"screw" = FUK

[Now back to Davie.]

We was now abowts 53° N of the *Line*, the Dayes very short, the Rain unending, & bitterlie Cold. We had indeed come out of our Long *Baye* by a Northerli intrance, suggesting that all this whyle the Land to our W was an immense *Island* running some 70 *Leagues* from N to S [Vancouver Island]. One *Daye* the Rain turn'd suddaynely to Snow. Wind was but light. We hove to, compleatly blinded by the dense Flakes, & for 4 Howres huddl'd belowe *Decks* till it relented. Luckily visibilitie return'd to us befor Darkness. We took our opportunitie, & got us into 1 of the many little *Bayes* along the *Coast* wich gave us safe *Harborage*, & none to soon, for now a Wind came out of the SW that, had it cau't us an Howre earlier, must unfailingly have dasht us up agaynst the Rocky *Shoare*.

This terrific Wind continu'd a Week, houling at all Howres, & brou't wt it drentching Raynes. Then at 4 a Clock one Morning we all awoke to dedd Calm, the *Shipp* still in the Water, no creaking or flapping of rigging. The *Watch* reportid that the black Clouds mov'd swiftlie of to the E, opening up a Star-fill'd skye & bright full *Moon*. By *Dawn*, wich did not come till passt 9 a Clock, a wind, much lighter than the last, came now out of the N, wich froze our *Bones* if we stood in it. The wett *Decks* turn'd to an Ice *Pond* for Skating, the rigging, the *Yards*, the *Masts* as if incas'd in clearest Glass, the very *Sea* Water abowte us was skimm'd o'er wt Ice, thou' I imagine it was onelie partially Salty water, for vast noisey Torrents of fresh Water was running off from half a doz. streams rushing of the *Land* & into the *Baye*. The mountaynes show'd a line of Snow starting at abowte 1,000 ft. Elevation. It was now neer *December*, we was got into a good *Shelter*, & thou't we wou'd make shift to Winter here.

There was many inlets & Rivers our *Botes* cou'd navigate, so we explor'd inland & found *ducks Gees* & *Swanns* plentifull, & the Rivers chok'd wt *Fish*, so we cou'd not lack for *Provender*. We had got but very little Wayes inland when we saw *Indians* in

Canoas. These evidenc'd grate surprise to see us—we was no dou't the 1st *White Men* here, & paddl'd of very quickly. Not kno'ing wether they was frendly, we at once return'd to the *Shipp*, & inform'd Mr *Mountague*, who prepar'd a force of *musketeers*, plus a caskitt of *ax*'s, *knives*, *beeds*, &c, & jin'd us, leaving a good *Gard* behind on the *Shipp*, & we proceeded up River, & presently found our Waye blockt by a *Flotilla* of 6 very big dug-out *Canoas*, wt highly painted & elaboratly carv'd *Bowes*, & abowte 30 *Indians* in each *Canoa*, arm'd wt *Speers* & *Bows* & *Arrows*. Our 2 *Botes* held onelie 15 *Men* each, but thou' vastly outnumber'd we was confident of the terrifying effeck of our *fire Arms* to route them if need be. However we had so farr on our Journie met onelie frendliness, & hop'd this wou'd continue. Mr *Mountage*, give him his Dew, is an utterlie Fearless *Man*, & after 1st instruckting his *men* they must on no account fire except the *Indians* attack us 1st, & then must discharge theire 1st shotts into the Ayr, to see if the *Indians* cou'd be frighted of before we was of necessity of taking Life, had just our *Bote* go forwards a bitt, & stood himself unarm'd in the *Bowe*, & wav'd smilingly in a frendly & beckning Manner. This was receiv'd by the most scouling stony silence, from the *Indians*. Mr *Mountigue*, now spoke in a frendly manner to the *Indians*, knowing they cou'd not understand his *Words*, but hoping his gentle address wou'd be well taken by em. Agayne, stony silence. Next, Mr *Mountague*, slowly bent doun & reech't into the *Caskitt* at his Feet. Wt 1 Motion, a 100 *Arrowes* was nockt into *Bows*. Mr *Mountague*, came up very slow, & at length show'd his *Hands & Arms* loaden wt bright colour'd strings of glass *Beeds*. Instantaneous relaxing of *Bow* Strings, follow'd by warm frendly Smiles.

All 6 *Canoas* begin to crowd up to us, but 1, who seem'd to be the *King*, in a larger & more elaborately payntid *Canoa*, shoutid out a long harangue at em, & tothers droppt back grumbling, so just he cou'd come up. They was dresst in what we had taken to be *furs*, but when they approacht cloas up to us, I cou'd see they was acktually of feathers, *Blowses* & *Trowsers* all of finely sown together skins of *Auks*, wich aboundid in these Waters, wich no dou't made a warm & waterproof *Raiment*, for I knew the Skins of these birds was very tough, & the feathers stiff & deep-pil'd, & cloas sett as Hairs.

When the *King* reacht to us, he very quicklie & greedilie graspt all that Mr *Mountague*, held, & snatcht it to him, & holding to the gun'l of our *Bote*, lookt in the *Caskitt* for more, but Mr *Mountague*, had wisely clos'd down the Lidd. The *Kings* broad Smyle at once turn'd back to a feirce Scoul, but seeing in a moment that no more *Beeds* was to be got this waye, he determin'd that more cou'd be gayn'd of us thro' a show of Frendship than thro' Threats, & laughing & haranguing in a jovial fashion (tho' his *Eys* never laught) he signal'd for us to follow, & his *Canoa* fell awaye from us, then begin paddling mightily upstream, follow'd by the others, & then by our own 2 *Botes*.

We shortlie reacht to a clear'd Area on the Banks of the River, on wich we cou'd see very long Wood *Howses*. The Banks was crowded wt *Men woemmen* & *Childern* come to gawp at us. Many *dogs* went in & out of theire Leggs, but no *Horses* or other *Cattel*. More *Canoas* was ty'd up to Poles out in the Water. Our *Guides* made fast theire *Canoas*, & walkt acrost a sort of Rickittie *Cat-Walk* from the poles over expos'd muddy Tide-Flat to the solid Ground. The *King* run very quicklie over the *Cat*-Walk to where we come up to make fast, & hinder'd our *Man* from tying up, gesticulating to Mr *Mountague*, & jabbring very quicklie, & often poynting to the *Caskitt*. We lookt at 1 tother in some pusslement, & suddaynely Mr *Mountague*, realiz'd what the *King* wou'd have, & reecht in the *Caskitt*, & drew out a little *Knife*, & give it to the *King*, who at once allow'd us to make fast. But then he hinder'd us from walking his gang-way to the Shoar, & Mr *Mountague*, handid him a tiny *Ax*, & he at once bad us all come ashoare. And then agayne, as we travers'd the *Cat-Walk*, in momentary daunger of braking thro' & sinking up to our *Necks* in Mudd at any rate, we was agayne stoppt short of the end, & the *King* poynting to the Ground at our *Feet*, & thence to himself, mayde

[98]

it playne to us that he own't this Ground, just as he own'd the Post to tye up at, & the Gang Way to come ashoar by, & we once more crosst his *Palm*, paying our *Toll* to set foot upon his *domain*.

Everywhere round us was signs of theire Welth, *Salmons* pil'd up like log Wood, wich they was gutting & putting into many *Hutches* for Smoaking, *Dear* Skins was everywhere, grate Mounds of shells of *Muscles* & giant *Cockels* & *snails* bigger than a *Mans* Fist. Tall Poles stood in clusters, wt fantastically carven faces of *Monsters* & *beests* 1 atop tother, & brilliantlie paynted; fancifull carving on the Roof peaks of theire long *Howses*, fine intricate basket-work everywhere; &, seen by the *Boyes* at once, whole *Howses* pil'd up wt *Ottor* Skins worth a *Kings Ransom* in *London*. We had expecktid to eke out a poor Meagre Winter, but now saw that we cou'd live here in some prosperitty.

A grate *Feast* was now forward, wt Roasts of *Venison* & *Bear* put on the fire, & shell *Fish* buri'd in the Embers. The smells was Delitious, & the *people* beginn eating wt Gusto, however when we envinc't some intrest in sharing theire *Repast*, the Food was firmlie withholden from us, wt much jabbring & poynting towards our *Bote*, & at length Mr *Mountague*, wt a Grimace of impatience, had 2 of the *Boyes* race back to the *Bote* & bring us more *Beeds* & *Mirrours* & hand *Ax*'s wherewith to purchase our *Dinner*.

After we eat, the *Indians* brou't out fine *Basketts* & fine Suits of *Cloaths* made of *Auks* Feathers, & especially brou't out *Ottors* Skins, & commenc't to trade em wt us, & the *Boyes* empti'd out their pockets of *Knives* & Balls of *Twine* & whate'er they cou'd muster, & begg'd Mr *Mountague*, for a share of the *Toys* in the *Caskitt*, wich he at 1st indulgentlie allow'd em, each a *Hand* full of *Trinkitts* & *gew-gaws*, & they traydid them so fast as they cou'd for more *Skins*, bewtifull rich & lustrous like the finest that cou'd be bou't at Terrifick Price in *London* from the *Russian* merchants, & the *Boyes* quicklie come back for more *Beeds*, but now Mr *Mountague*, sharplie rebuff'd em, & said they had had enough from him, that the *Trinkitts* was to finance the *Tripp*, (& I saw he had his own *Ey* on the fine *Skins*,) & now he beginn trading himself, & pil'd up severall doz. of *Skins*, & all we saw about us was covetese & Greed writ in large Letters on each *Countenance* a both Sides, & I noted Dr Harris, standing Of[f] aside grinning Sardonically at the *Scene*, nor cou'd I jine him wt too good *Conscience*, for wt my silver *knife fork* & *Spoon*, & 2 Gold finger *Rings*, worth abowte a *gn.*, I had myself purchas'd 20 good *Skins*.

The *Boyes* markt theire purchases & stow'd em in the *Botes*, but wt much loud grumbling at the captaynes large Share. We had neer given up all our *Dross* now, & had neer taken all theire *Skins*. Indeed the *Ottors* was numbrous in the *Bayes*, but cost us grate difficultie to take e'en 1 of em, since we lackt skill, & had no *Harpoons*, & if we shot em, they meerlie sank to the Bottom.

The *Indian Village* was at the forward Edg of a long open playne beside the River, perhaps swept clear of Gyant *Trees* by repeatid Flooding, for the *Indians* poor wooden *Hatchetts* cou'd ne'er have clear'd em. At the far Edg of the Playne, a herd of 50 *Staggs* [elk] was grazing peecefullie. We had watcht em, & commented on theire large size & handsomeness whylst we was eating, & wonder'd that they stay'd ther wt impunity, when the many *Dear* & *Bear* Skins abowte show'd us these *Indians* was capable of taking large *Game*. After the flurrie of frantick Trayding had been concluded, some of us walkt over towards em, to have a better look, poynting to em, & then to the *Indians Bows*, to ask em why they didnt hunt em. They shook theire *Heads* & held out theire *Arms* to signify theire helplessness to do so, & we soon saw why. A few of em, to show us, took theire heaviest *Bows*, & walkt cautiously towards the big *Animals*. These latter liftid theire *Heads* to observe em, & when they had got abowte 200 ft. from em, wich is to say, effecktive *Bow* range, the *Staggs* calmlie walkt of a 100 ft., & then commenc't grazing agayne. Evidentlie the *Staggs* favor'd the open country for theire Grazing, but since they shar'd it wt the *Indians*, they had learn'd wt grate exactitude the distance from wich an *Arrow* was daungerous, &, keeping that distance, & keeping a wary *Ey* on the *Indians*, new they had nothing more to fear.

[100]

We had of course pracktically the intire *Village* wt us, watching us wt Curiosity, & since we had determin'd to remayne here for the Winter, we saw a chaunce now to impress em wt our *Power*, in order that they wou'd respeck us, & not feel theire superior Nos. gave em leave to tyrannize o'er us. Because I am consider'd a fair Marksmen, Mr *Mountague*, had a *Muskett* charg'd wt 3 heavy *Bullets*, & gave it me & told me to try to bring down the biggist *Stagg*. I took it, signalling the *King* to accompany me, & the 2 of us approcht so neer to a big *Stagg* as we cou'd, befor I judg'd he was abowte to withdraw. At that poynt, the *King* & the *Stagg* both observing me curiously, I rested the *Barrell* of my peice on a fork'd Staff, took very carefull aym, & fir'd into the *Creatur's* Throat. I had the satisfacktion to see it stumble, fall to its *Foreleggs*, & roll over. I turn'd back, & saw the *King* lying as if Dead beside me. I then turn'd full round, & saw the rest of the *Indians* froze in deathlie stillness, *Mowthes* droopt, *Eys* popping out, & in another Instant they had droppt everything & turn'd & was running full tilt awaye from us.

* * *

J now had to go in to the clinic once a month, to have a urine sample checked, a blood sample, and to be prodded, fingered, and felt up by the doctors. From the time she left the car, went in, waited in the waiting room, and finally had her check-up and came out again, usually about an hour would pass. The clinic was on the edge of the city, adjoining an area of several acres of young second-growth alder, intermixed with a few fairly large Douglas firs. There was a network of trails through it, and, though it wasn't terrific birding habitat, George usually spent the hour skulking around in it, for discipline setting himself a goal of twenty species of birds he had to see or hear in that time. He usually just made it, though at first, in the winter months, it took considerable pishing. "Pishing" is a strange behavior practiced mainly by American birders. You stand by a likely looking bit of thick brush or overgrown marsh, where, perhaps, there is no sign at all of birdlife, and you begin making this hissing, rasping sound like *Pissh pissh pissh*. You do it very loudly (first making sure no human beings are within earshot), and small birds come flushing out of the brush, chipping and scolding, and close in on you often from as far as a hundred yards away. Some birds, particularly wrens and kinglets, the tiniest of birds, will all but land on your nose, in a paroxysm of fury or curiosity. He had done it out in an open field in late summer, and suddenly had the air almost darkened with swarms of swallows filling the sky above him. He'd had owls and hawks, and once a fox, approach him with an almost frightening rush. Nobody knows why this sound has this effect. Roger Tory Peterson theorized that it was the sound an owl makes when it is about to cast up a pellet, and it is certainly true that small birds will always gather around an owl if they spot one, and scold and harass it to the best of their abilities. Anyway, it is often quite magical in its effects. Sometimes he would go into the woods on a particularly gloomy dripping day, and there would be no sound, no trace, of bird life, not even the clicking of a winter wren. He would start pishing, and suddenly he would be surrounded by winter and Bewick's wrens, robins and varied thrushes, golden-crowned and ruby-crowned kinglets, black-capped and chestnut-backed chickadees, Steller's jays, juncos, white-crowned and golden-crowned sparrows, an odd wintering Hutton's vireo, a downy woodpecker, dozens of song sparrows, a creeper, a red-breasted nuthatch—and there, standing in that one spot, he would have seventeen of his twenty species. From then on it was no trouble to pick up the other three. He would usually hear a crow cawing somewhere, and watching openings in the sky, see a glaucous-winged gull fly over. Then it was just a question of picking up a house sparrow or starling back around the clinic.

As they got into spring and early summer, the appointments now came two weeks apart, but each time they came, the make-up of the bird population would be different, as winter birds left the area for their summer territories, at the same time that new birds moved in, either to nest, or pass on through to the north. And now, of course, the birds were all singing, which made them much easier to find. He would walk through the trails hardly even looking (indeed, the leaves were out thicker and thicker each day, so that he couldn't, in the dense scrub, see more than a few feet at any rate), but easily picking up his twenty species and more by listening to the songs.

Everything went beautifully until the last couple of months. He was waiting by the car one day when J came out, and he could see she was keeping herself calm only with great effort.

"There's a complication," she said, and got in the car and sat down, looking straight ahead. He got in next to her, and waited.

"He was feeling my stomach all over, like he usually does, and listening with his stethoscope, but today he felt around for a much longer time, and finally he said 'Well, what do you know, it's decided to turn upsidedown.' "

He listened, not quite understanding.

"He says that means it'll be a breech birth, and probably it'll have to be Caesarian. I'm sorry, but you'll have to wait a little longer. I have an appointment now to go over and have an X-ray."

"I'll go with you," he said.

"I knew everything was going too well."

"That's okay. You've got really good doctors. They'll know just what to do."

The sun was shining brightly.

"He says it's surprisingly common, five in a hundred, or something like that. Wouldn't you know I'd be one of the five. You don't think about those statistical things, unless it suddenly turns out to be you."

"Well obviously," he said, "it's nicer to have everything go perfectly, but on the other hand, Caesarian is really the easy way to have a child. It's so routine they do it in about five minutes. You just go to sleep, wake up, and there it is, perfectly formed

[103]

and beautiful, whereas everyone else has to go through hell for about fourteen hours, with all that straining and pain, and getting ripped up, and then it comes out with its head twisted out of shape, and so on."

"I guess that's true," she said. "I admit I wasn't looking forward to that part."

While they were waiting in the X-ray room, J saw one of the nurses she knew from the clinic.

"Hi, how's it going?" the nurse said.

"Well, a bit more complicated than it was. It seems it's going to be born breech."

"Oh really," the nurse said, smiling. "It's surprising how common that is. We had one just this morning. We call them our 'ballerinas.' They always come out with the legs up over their heads, and they stay that way for about twelve hours, before they come down. It really looks comical. But they're always the most beautiful babies. When the head doesn't come out first, it doesn't get squeezed up so much, so it's always a beautiful shape right from the start."

"I'm having an X-ray to see if it might have to be Caesarian."

"Oh, that's the easy way. Instead of never knowing when you'll have to rush to the hospital, you just make an appointment, come in and have it in a few minutes, and in a couple of days you're home, and, I guarantee, not nearly so sore afterwards. When I had my last baby I couldn't sit down comfortably for a week."

"My wife's such a chicken," he said, "I knew she'd find some easy way to do it."

They all laughed.

After they had been home for about an hour, the doctor called. J talked to him briefly, and when she hung up, she came over to him smiling broadly. "He's seen the X-rays, and he says I can go ahead and just have it, they won't have to operate."

They held each other, both of them with tears of relief in their eyes.

[104]

* * *

[Davie:]

We are at the end of *February*. I have had no Tyme to keep up this *Journal*. Instedd of the long Bleak Winter huddl'd below *Decks* that we had anticipated, this has instedd been 1 of the most interesting Winters of my *Life*, all to speedily departing.

For 1 thing, in our *Travells* heretofore, much closer to the *Line*, we had no need to stop for Winter, since ther *was* no Winter in the ordinary Meaning, & so we ne'er stopt at 1 *Place* for longer then a Week, or at most cloas to a Month once or twice. Now here we have been for severall Months, & have had our best opportunitie to really kno' a *Place*. Secondlie, Winter has prov'd in the mayne as mild as Winters at *Home*, thou' on occassion extreamly stormie, but never extreamly cold. The *Pattern* wou'd be for a week or 10 Dayes, powerfull Winds out of the SW bringing drentching Rain, but Mild Temperature. This to be succeeded by Wind from the N, & very Cold, for several Dayes, but also cleer & Sunny. Onelie twice or thrice was ther Snow of any Amount, & that gone in a few Dayes. And, as I have befor said, ther were open *Areas* in-land, esp. alongside of the River, & also Sandy *Beeches* expos'd at Low Tides along the *Coast*, giving us a chaunce to make long Walks along the *Shoar*, & also to penitrate in Land for severall Myles. As a consequence, my *Natural History* collections was built up enormously, wt doz. of Kinds of *Mosses* & *Liver Worts* & *Ferns*, wch flourish'd here in as grate profusion as any Tropickal *Forrest*. Also I took some 20 severall Kinds of warm-blouded *Animals*, & neer to 150 kinds of *Land Birds*, including 5 Kinds of *Owl*—the Grate White *Owl* [Sncwy Owl]; *American* Tawny *Owl* [he must mean the Spotted Owl, now rare. I've never seen one]; Little *Owl* [Saw-whet Owl? Pigmy Owl?]; *Eagel Owl* [Great Horned Owl]; *Scops Owl* [probably Screech Owl, though Flammulated Owl is a possibility]; 5

[105]

kinds of *Buzzard* [although in this country, "buzzard" colloqui-
ally refers to vultures, he uses it in the more technical sense, to
refer to the stocky, medium to large sized open country hawks of
which the Red-tailed Hawk is the commonest representative—
hawks of the genus *Buteo*. Although he claims to have collected
five, only two species are really likely where he is: Red-tailed
Hawk and Rough-legged Hawk. However I have seen rough-legs
in a bewildering variety of plumages, from almost pure white, to
jet black, so likely he is putting down these different plumages as
different species, an easy mistake to make]; *Goshawks, sparrow
hawks* [he would mean Sharp-shinned or Cooper's Hawks], *Gyr
Faulcons, partridges* [probably Ruffed and Blue Grouse]; & many
Kinds of *Finches, Wrens*, & *Thrushes* [these last three names were
used so generally then, that they could refer to almost any birds.
No doubt his 150 species includes several, like the hawks, which
are merely color phases, or different plumages of the same
species, but even so, it is an astonishingly good number of land
birds for mid winter at this latitude, and shows what a good
hunter and field naturalist Davie is. Was].

Unfailinglie, a *Band* of *Indians* accompani'd any of us, when
ever we was a Field, & just so soon as I shott a *Bird*, or *Animal*, or
even pickt a strip of *Moss*, I was told it belong'd to em, & had to
pay em for 't. One *Saylor* complayn'd to me that he pickt up a
flatt Stone to skipp it along the River, & an *Indian* at once
attempted to charge him for 't! My gratest problem in setting out
a long colleckting *Journy* was the inconvenience of carrying
enough *Trinkitts* in the pocket to Pay for whatever we chaunc't
upon. However, whilst this was a meer annoyance for the others,
I manag'd to bring it to my Proffit. One thing the *Indians* neg-
leckted to sell was theire own *Speech*, wch is what they had,
perhaps, of most valew to me. Throu' constant asking em the
Name of each thing we encounter'd, & secretly writing it down, I
quicklie accumulated a Vocabulary of severall 100 *Words*, & a
rudamentary Grammer, & soon found myself able to ask em (my
Questions eek'd out wt many Gestures) simple things abowte

theire *Lives*, & abowte the *Natural History* of the *Land*, at wich they was very expert. It seems the vast & unfailing runs of *Fish*, esp. *Salmons* & *Trouts*, coming up the Rivers, the countless Sea *Birds* in Autumn & Winter, the abundant *Game* & *roots* & *Berries* of Summer, the Mild Climate, made Life so effortless for em, they devoted most of the Tyme to making elaborate wood *carvings*, & to weaving exquisite *Baskitts*. These *carvings*, highly Paynted, & the *Baskitts* was design'd for no pracktical Purpose, but was meant meerly to display theire *Welth*, & when, after a Year of steddy Work, they had accumulated so much *Welth* they had no more Room in theire *Buildings* to Stoar it, they wou'd wait for a stretch of calm Weather in mid Summer, & pile it to the Skies aboard theire special *Cargo Canoas*, & the whole *Tribe* wou'd make a visit to some neighbouring *Tribe*, not, as you might imagine, to sell or Trayde theire *Goods*; but rather, after a period of Feasting & haranguing, the *King*, claiming all this communal work of the *Tribe* as his own Propetty, wou'd, in a Magnificent Gesture, *Give* it all to the *King* of the other *Tribe*, after wich they wou'd leave, & return to theire *Village* here. In fact, 1 Reason they was so madd to get theire *Hands* on our *Beeds* &c. was to help em in theire accumulation of *Booty* for the next *Visit* they wou'd make.

From what we had come to learn of these *Indians*, the last we wou'd have suspeckted was an eeleemosinary Streak, & I askt em this over & over to be certayne I had understood, that all was meerly *given* to the other *Tribe*. Indeed it was so, & they ne'er weari'd of telling me of past *Visits*, & when they got to the Part where the *King*, wt a wonderful Flourish, gave away the *Tribes* Yeers Labour, they fell to laughing so hard *Teers* made furroughs in the dirt of theire *Faces*, & at length they fell to the ground & clutcht theire *Stomacks*, & shook till we feer'd they was made ill. Little & by Little it came out, that they was but ill reciev'd by theire *neighbours* when they come wt theire grate *Treasur*, that thou' perforce they was given grate & elaborate feesting, the others but ill disguis'd theire scouls & frowns & unhappiness to

[107]

see em. And for why? Because,—& here is the explanation for all,—the Iron-bound *Law* was that this visited *Tribe* must now prepare a *Return* Visit, in wich they must make a *return* Gift, & inless this Gift was many times larger & more opulent then the Gift they had that Daye reciev'd, they wou'd be forever disgrac'd amongst all the *Tribes* up & down the *Coast!* so the Gift after all was but *Money* put out to Intrest.

Dr *Harris*, as I knew he wou'd, however, did not allow me to rest wt my satirical comments abowte the *Indians*, for 't was but to obvious our own *men* was no whit behind em in avarice & Greed. Our *Boyes* quicklie taught the *Indians* the use of Pipes & *Tobacco*, & then commenc't to trade of theire own meagre Stoars of *Tobacco* (intailing upon themselves Months or Yeers perhaps of deprivation if they us'd up the small amount remayning to em), in order to get more *Ottor* Skins. They had alreddy traded awaye every Thing they own'd, & all that was not firmlie attacht to the *Shipp*. Indeed we beginn to notice the *Indians* covering theire dri'd *Fish* wt cuttings from our Best spare *Sayles*, & Mr *Mountague*, had at length to address em quite sternly, wt promises of severe Punishments for any cau't stealing *Sayles* & *Rigging* that may be needed to save our Lives 1 Daye. Partickularly, he was fearfull that the *Indians* wou'd get possession of some of our *Musketts*, for after theire initial Terrour of em, they soon grew us'd to em, & made it cleer they very much wanted to get theire *Hands* on these mirackle *Weapons*. But we had never felt easy wt em, or thou't we cou'd trust em very Far, & being vastlie outnumber'd by em, we fear'd that if they had an equalitie of *Fire Power* wt us; our Lives wou'd be little Worth.

* * *

On a beautiful day in mid-spring they came in for a check-up. It was in fact the day the baby was due, though it was giving no signs whatever of coming. J went into the waiting room, and he

[108]

started off for the paths through the woods. When they had come three days before he had found, just within the margin of the woods, a song sparrow with a broken back, perhaps struck by a car and bounced into the woods at this spot. It was alert and perfectly healthy, except for the fact that the legs and tail dragged limply, and the bird couldn't get into flight, but sort of rowed itself along the ground with its wings. It was just off the path in a patch of dry last-year's weeds. George could see that the bird, not wasting time feeling sorry for itself, had eaten all the seeds from these weeds. The bird was in perfect breeding plumage, the feathers shining rich brown and gray and black in the sun. He picked it up and moved it to another patch of weeds with more seeds, and where the bird would be a bit more concealed in taller foliage.

Now coming by the area again, he found what remained of the bird. Bright rufous feathers were scattered across the path, and the bird's carcass, the breast and one side eaten, was under a bush, where it had been caught by a rat or some other small animal. It was what he had expected, and was for the best since the bird could not have survived. He was not upset by the natural process.

However for some reason he did not go far, or spend much time in the wood, and when he came out, J was already waiting by the car.

"He says to go home and get my stuff and check in tonight. They're going to do a Caesarian tomorrow morning."

* * *

[Davie]

Every *Man* aboard own'd enough in *Ottor* Furrs to give him a small Fortune in the *London* Markets; & now came Mutinous Murmurs, scarce disguis'd, of giving o'er our will-o'- the-wisp

Errand of finding a NW Paysage, & making straiht for *Home*. This gather'd Ground untill 1 Daye a *Man* nam'd *Jeffries*, a Hard Case, & 1 of those who had jumpt *Shipp* on the *Isle* of *Woemmen*, & begg'd to come back, & been graciously forgi'n by Mr *Mountague*, suddaynlie fac't up to the Capt.; & said in no uncertayn Terms: "That the *Boys* wou'd refuse to pull a *Line*, or turn a *Watch*, till the Capt. agreed to sett Coarse for *London*". The *Boyes* stood firm & Brazen behind him, foregettfull of all the Capt.'s goodnesse to em, & it lookt like a very frightening Pass we had come to, but Mr *Mountague*, is nothing if not an active & Courageous *Man*, & he staukt straiht up to this Miscreant, & fell'd him wt a single Bloe of his *Fist*, & commandid the *Officers* to cast him in Iron, wch they did forthwith, & all so quyck & decisive the Back was Broaken of the *Mutiny* before it had well begun, wch is the onelie Waye, & Mr *Mountague*, having shewn his strength, at once shew'd his Mercie (to the Others, not to the *Ring Leader*,) by speaking Kindlie & forgivinglie to em, & explayning that they was got so Farr, the NW Paysage, wch he expecktid to find direcklie, was by a good Deal theire shortist Waye back. The *Boyes*, reliev'd to have got of so easie for theire *Mischiefe*, Agreed to this wt a *Huzzah* & *Caps* threwn in the Ayr, & we stockt up wt Victual, & sett our Coarse N. We shortlie found our Waye blockt by the *Main*, & beginn to trend W, wch we continu'd for fully 300 *Leagues*, & beginn to dispair of finding a Pathe to the N. Fresh Victual was exhaustid, & the season rushing on, we cou'd ill afford to stop & hunt the abundant *Game*, but made our best Waye on Hard *Tack* & *Biskitts*, & the familiar sign's of *Scurvie* made their apparence. At last we struck an opning to the N, & soon made into a shallow flat-bottom'd *Sea*, wch was *Behrings* Sea, discover'd by the *Russians*, & now we had some manner of *Charts* to follow. It was Miserable & grey & rainy, but so far not stormie, & we made good Waye, the Capt. driving on Daye & Nigt like a *Demon* to get us thro' befor the Winter Pack Ice clos'd in, & we had to wait on another Year, & now we beginn to lose *men* in earnest; & Dr *Harris*, tol'd him in

Private that we must stop & take in fresh Food, else we wou'd lose all.

't Was now Midd-*June* & we was 69 degrees N of the *Line*. We putt in behind the shelter of a *Hedd-Land*, & as luck wou'd have it, chaunc't direckly upon an *Indian Village*. They was fatt sturdie looking *Indians* in tiny frayle looking *Canoas* made of skins sewn together, wch they paddl'd wt grate skill, & they was dresst cap-a-pie in skins, covring all but theire *Faces*, wich was Jollie & grinning. They paddl'd straiht up to us as if not surpris'd by our apparence, & begin to hayle us, calling us over & over a name: *Kosiki*; & Dr *Harris*, smoakt it at once, & said: Theyre Calling us "Cossacks", the *Russian* furr trayders have been here. Dr *Harris*, had liv'd as a young *Man*, in *Saint Petersburgh*, & beginn to speak to the *Indians* in the *Russian* tongue, wch they seem'd to understand, & answer'd him back a few Words, the meaning of wich is, "We was cordially invited to come ashoar".

*   *   *

The doctor had checked J and she had dilated 1 millimeter, but otherwise was showing no progress, and the baby was now over nine pounds and still growing, and already really too big for a safe breech delivery. George noticed that J, who could be so exasperatingly weepy and trembley over a small illness, was now absolutely calm. She had cooked dinners for him, and frozen them, and put labels on each with cooking directions. She had made dinners for seven nights, which was more than necessary, but she thought perhaps she wouldn't feel much like cooking when she first got back.

He brought her in, carrying her overnight bag, and they checked in, and were shown her room. It looked pleasant enough, and no one was occupying the other bed. The nurse said they wanted to begin preparing her, so it would be better if he left. He kissed J, and held her for a minute, but she was obviously calm, and said she would be all right, and got out her book to read, and so he left.

He drove home slowly, often stopping in wooded areas to listen for owls. It was something he didn't normally do. It was part of his sudden new freedom.

He arrived at the empty, silent house, and put the kettle on to make a cup of coffee. He turned on the radio, but at night during the summer a San Francisco station came in on top of the Canadian station, so he turned it off. The house seemed even quieter.

My bachelor freedom, he thought.

He listened to the kettle ticking and hissing, and finally got up and made himself a cup of coffee.

* * *

[Davie:]

I have been grately behind *Hand* in keeping up this, my *Diary*, but onelie every *Month*, or so, writing in summary fashion, that wich has passt. Althou' we commenc't here, one of the most Deleightful *Sojourns* of my *Life*, when we anchor'd our *Shipp*, we was in very poor Condition. The *Men* was very bad wth *Scurvie*, loosing theire *Teeth*, & wt terrible soars on theire *Leggs*, & much loss of Life, so that we was down to 32 *Men*. Dr *Harris*, Mr *Mountague*, *Jemmie* the Cabbin *Boye*, & I, had all far'd somewhat better, I am certayne purely by Virtue of Dr *Harris's* theory, that the cause of *Scurvie* was absense of fresh victual, for, I am asham'd now to say, we eat somewhat better than the ordinary *Seemen*, & when *Seabirds*, as oft chaunc't, came aboard, & I collecktid em for Speciments, Dr *Harris*, insistid, that we eat the *Meat* of em, however poor & oylie.

Most of the *Indians* spoke but a Phrase or 2 of *Russian*, Dr

[112]

Harris, said, but one, the *Chief* amongst em, spoke it quite well, & this was very helpfull to us. The first he told us, was that we cou'd at any rate have got but little wayes farther N, as the pack Ice had not yet broak up, & wou'd not do so for another Month or 2, *if then*, since it did not break up at all some Yeers. But, he said, this was theire flourishing time o' Yeer, so they cou'd easilie keep us here till the Ice shou'd clear. He said that we was got into very safe *harborage*, & 't was besides past the period of Feirce *Storms*, wch they get on the changing of the Seasons. This was all good News to us (except abowte the Ice not always breaking up, tho' he said that was but Rare,) & we come ashoar, & at once a grate *Feest* was forward, & continu'd for some Dayes, whilst our *Boyes* vy'd wt the *Indians* for who cou'd perform the gratist prodigies of eatting, & the *Scurvie* meltid awaye like majick, wich Dr *Harris*, said, was proof of his theorie, but wich Mr *Mountague*, who had alwayes seem'd jealous of that Theorie, disagreed wt, & said he thou't it was a special cordial or balm in the *oyl* & *Greece* of the *Seals* & *sea Horses* [walrus] & *Sea Birds* we eat. The *Village* was but poor in Apparence, an expanse of bare, sodden Mud reeking of *Fish* intrayles & the ordure of dozaynes of yipping *Dogs* ty'd up all abowte. Excep where they had trod it into a Quagmyre, the *Ground* was still half cover'd wt dingey Snow. Theire *dwellings* was severall large Communal *Buildings* of mud & bark on frames of Sticks. Everywhere tame abowte our Feet & eating of Offal, as do the *Kites* in our Countrie, was the most inmackulate Pure White *Gulls*, wich, when flying agaynst the white skie or snowy Banks all but vanisht, & seem'd to be meerlie theire dark *Eys* & *bills* moving. It was the first of this *Kind* we had seen, & I collecktid some, to the amusement of the *Indians*, who cou'd not see what I wantid wt such poor Fare. [Davie is describing Ivory Gulls, a high arctic species which can still be seen scavenging around Esquimo villages.] These was the most chearfull *Indians* I had ever seen, apparentlie content to feest everie Daye of theire lives, altho' they tol'd us ther was many Lean times as well, wich is why they made the most of theire bountie now. As our *Saylors* gain'd strength, it did not take em long to realize the *Indian Men* was as genrous wt their *Wyves* as these *wyves* was wt theire Charmes. The *Boyes* liv'd aboard the *Shippe*, where the *Indians* (& especially theire *Woemmen*,) regularly visit'd them. Dr *Harris*, & I, liv'd in the *Village*, & after a Daye or 2, *Jemmie* the Cabbin *Boye* also, who Dr *Harris*, borrow'd of Mr *Mountague*, so we cou'd have him as a *Valet*. The *building* was quite large inside, & partlie broak up into seperate *Dwellings*, tho' most fairly expos'd, so 't was onelie really private at Nigt, or Twiligt, rather, (for the Sun ne'er quite went down,) when it wou'd be very Dark inside the Window-less *Howse*. But the *Indians* was little concern'd wt Privacie, & seem'd content to live theire lives befor all who shou'd care to look. For to beginn, as they inter'd the *Dwelling*, in a sort of outer *Hallwaye*, they divestid themselvs of muddie *Bootes* & clothes, & strippt more or less Nakkid, befor intring the flickring half-light of the Fire in the center of the *Howse*. The *Howse* was so warm, & this seem'd so Natural, that befor many Dayes we did it ourselvs, wt out a tho't. Then more feesting, & much telling of *Jokes* & *Tales*, wich they lov'd very much; & wich the *Chief* translatid into *Russian* for Dr *Harris*, who then translatid em into *English* for me, the *Indians* all watching Dr *Harris*, to see if he smyl'd, when the poynt was made cleer to him, & then watching me, to see if I smyl'd in my turn, when he had recountid it to me, & all this marvellously jovial & cheerfull. The *Woemmen* was not shov'd to the back Ground as in other peopples we had visited, but play'd a Part equal to the *Men*, & ther was much toying of the *Men* & *Woemmen* wt each other, (tho' this most wt *Husbandes* & *Wyves*,) & they wou'd withdraw a little apart from us, tho' still in Vuw if we car'd to look in that direcktion, whylst they ingag'd in theire Amrous *Exercizes*.

Dr *Harris*, sho'd his disgust of this carousing, & stay'd back out of the Waye to sleep wt *Jemmie* in a far Corner, & also spent much Tyme, teaching him to read & write, wich he pickt up wt grate Facility. There was a very young *Girl* nam'd *Deedeea*, who sho'd that she wish'd to be frendlie to me, & bro't me special bits

[114]

of *Meat*, &c., all of wich I eat to be polite, tho' her ideas of delitiousness was often the embryo of an *Auk* soak'd in oyl for a Yeer, & to show me how cleanly & fastidious she was, she wou'd wash her *Hair* before me—in a bowl of *Urine* she had sav'd for the Purpose! but I was anxious to learn the *Language*, & she was very patient of giving me the name, & pronouncing it over & over till I cou'd say it, of each thing abowte the *Howse*, so I cou'd write it in my *Book*. She had shining high *Cheeks* & bright *Eys* & a merry *Smyle*, & some thing in her carriage, tho' they was little alike but for theire Youth, put me in mind of my young *Wife* lost in *Child Birth*, & since their *Names* was so alike, I insensibilie came to call her *Debby*. Modester then the other *Woemmen*, she wore a kind of *Shift* to cover her bodie in the *Howse*. But one Daye when all was out of Doors but us, & we was got into a private Corner, & had run out of Things abowte the *Howse* for her to name for my *Language* notes; I poyntid to her tiny *Nose*, & she gave me the name of it, & then her *Eers*, & then her *Fingers*, & *Hands*, & *Knees*, & then very sweetlie & innocentlie, she pull'd up her *Shift* over her *Hedd*; & poyntid out to me the *Partes* of her *Bodie*, & had me touch em one by one, whilst I said the *Name*, to be sure I had learnt them properlie, & a force took hold of me that I cou'd no more resist then I could stop my breathing; & from that Daye we liv'd as *Man* & *Wife*.

*

A nurse told him he had a son, and if he came to the door of the operating room, they would be bringing out the baby in a minute, and he could see it briefly. He waited where he was told, and the baby in a portable incubator was wheeled out, and he walked along beside it—him—looking in at him, and though he had prepared himself to see something wrinkled and misshapen and bright purple, the baby looked quite big and handsome and well formed, and was quite absorbed in kicking its legs. The pediatrician was striding along beside them quite cheerfully.

"Everything's fine," he said. "You've got a regulation baby with just the right number of fingers and toes and so on. I'm going to check him thoroughly now, but from my preliminary check he's just fine. They're just finishing up with your wife, and she looks very happy. You'll be able to see her in a few minutes." A nurse now led him down to a hallway where he could look through a glass partition and see all the newly delivered babies, those just born that day in portable incubators, the others side by side in tiny cribs. In a few minutes his child, he already recognized him, was wheeled in to take his place alongside the others. The baby was sleeping quietly now. As a purely objective scientist, he had to confess that he was a great deal bigger and handsomer than any of the others.

Well, there it is, he thought, a new generation. He will live well into the next century. What will it be like? They say kids have to react against their parents and be just the opposite from them in order to have their own personalities, so perhaps he will grow up hating wildlife, which will be just as well. Maybe he'll grow up being on different kinds of teams, and belonging to different organizations, and perhaps he'll be an inner city accountant, part of a big corporation. God speed him whatever he does. The day for people like me is pretty much gone, living out on the fringes of things, with my pre-industrial mentality.

Now he was ushered in to see J. She was smiling. An I-V tube went into her arm. A catheter tube came out from under the sheets, and emptied into a polythene bag. "I can't eat for a few days, because the anaesthetic might make me sick, and I would burst my stitches."

"He's very handsome," George said. "I'm beginning to wonder who the father is."

"He really is pretty good. You should have heard him yell when they took him out. He's got a real pair of lungs."

"How was it?"

"It was pretty nice, really. They only gave me a spinal, so I was fully awake. I was a little nervous at first, but they gave me some gas to relax me, and after that I quite enjoyed it. They said I could have a mirror and watch, but I passed on that. But I could hear the snip snip snip of the scissors. It was all very casual. The anaesthesiologist spent the whole time with me chatting about Britain, where he had been stationed in the army. The two doctors spent their time talking about sailing. They both have boats. The delivery only took a minute. The lengthy part was slowly cutting through each layer and tying off the arteries. It was funny listening to them: 'Gosh, look at the size of that bladder,' and to realize it was *me* they were talking about. Then one of them said, 'It's a boy,' and I heard this loud sucking squelching sound, and they pulled him out, followed by this terrifically loud wailing. And then there was a very long time while they hooked me back up, and sewed me up, layer by layer."

* * *

[Davie:]

't Was now the brief *Flowring* Time in this far Northern *Land*, under the constant Rayes of the Midnight Sun. The surface of the *Land* thaw'd, & stunted *Lings* & *Hethers* bloom'd, & *Ducks* & *Geese* & *Wading Birds* by the countless 1,000s nestid acrost the Treeless *playnes*, wich ths *Indians* call'd "Toondra", wich Dr *Harris*, said, was in fact a *Russian* Word, signifying Water Meadow. The *Indian Woemmen* was busy Daye & Nigt (since ther was no Nigt,) gathring *Birds Egs*, most from *Sea Birds* on off-shoare *Towers* of Rock, wich *Egs* they pil'd into tight vessels made of ingeniously sew'd together *Skins*, & they cover'd over these *Egs* with *Oyl*, wch, they told us, preserv'd the *Egs* like New, for upwards of a Yeer, & even give us some to eat, wich they had from Last Yeer, & they was as fresh as if ta'en that Daye. The *Indian Boyes* was busy wth theire ingenious dedd-fall *Traps*, wt wch they took *Lemming*, & the small pure whyte *Foxes*

[117]

that aboundid. The men daily went out in theire tiny *Canoas*, & wt theire long *harpoons*, feerlesslie attackt giant *Sea Horses*, & the smaller *Wales*, esp. a very Fatt white *Wale* of abowte 10 feet Long. We regularly went out wt the hunting parties in our *Pinace*, wt wch we cou'd easier dragg back the *Catch* of the Daye, & also wt our *Musketts*, wch they knew of from the *Russians*, but didnt have any of, we cou'd help them to take daungerous pray, esp. the giant white *Bears*.

One Daye when we was out thus, we met some *Indians* who had been farther N, & they tol'd us the Pack Ice was preparing to brake up. We quicklie made all Ready, & sett *Sayle*. The *Indians* we was staying wt generously give us all the *Food* they had lay'd in thus far, saying they cou'd easilie replenish 't. The *Chief*, who knew the most *Russian*, cou'd not accompany us for a *Guyde* this busy time of Yeer, but since I had made shift, now, to converse very well wt *Debbie*, & she knew ths countrie very well, it was agree'd she wou'd come wt us.

The *Chief* especially cou'd not leave his *People* just now, as many of the *Men* was down wt a Suddayne illness, like a *Cold*, but more severe, wch they call'd the *Russian* sickness, since, the onlie Time they experienc't illness was when the *Russians* visited em. Dr *Harris*, sayde those afflicktid, shou'd remayne at *Home*, & dress theire warmist, & remayne cloas to the Fire, so to swett copiouslie, & therbye Purge the surfeit of *Fluids*. To help them—who had helpt us grately—we left them 3 *Musketts*, & a supplie of *Powder* & *Shott* wch, if martiall'd, shou'd last em thro' the Season. *Debbie* herself was quite alarmingly Sick by now, wt much phlegm & coughing, & seering Fever, tho' Dr *Harris*, purg'd & bledd her, & as much as possible we kept her Warm, & out of Chills, & fixt her nourishing *Broths*. She still, wrappt in Furrs, insistid on coming on *Deck* to act as our *Guyde*, telling us to stear cloas into the *Coast*, wch was deep *Channel'd* & free of Rocks, & wich, because of the *Tide* Race, is where the Ice wou'd brake up first.

We ran before light Winds for 2 Dayes, befor we saw the

"Blink", a white flashing on the Horizon that indicated the approach of the Pack Ice. We went up & down along the Edg of the pack, wch rumbl'd & crackt, & shiftid & crasht to the Water most terrifyingly, but almost as soon as we arriv'd, an off *Shoar* wind carri'd it out, opning wide *Leads* for us, & cautiously we workt our way N, & then, on a Daye, the *Land* gave awaye, & we turn'd E, & *Debbie* say'd this was as far as the *Land* extendid to the N, & we had indeed come to the Topp of this grate *Continent*, & now, *God* willing, & Ice retreating, cou'd sayle direck for the *Colonies*!

And as daylie the Ice drove farther awaye, the very best News of all: *Debbies* helth seem'd to mend by the Daye, & she was soon well out of Daunger.

* * *

I am the chief so I must decide.

Everybody is sick with the Cossack sickness. I am very sick. Nobody wants to go out and hunt. But food is running out. We gave all our extra food to the Cossacks. We are very hungry. I don't want to hunt either, but somebody has to do something or we will starve, and I am the chief. "Mukje," I say, "you stupid lazy woman seal, you doodly bird, why do you lie there gasping and drooling when there is good walrus hunting? Let's go." He tries to get up, but is not very strong. I help him up. "You are right," he says. "Why am I lying here? Let's go." I help him get his furs on, and we go through the village and find five more men who are strong enough to go. "But if we get out to the walrus herd, how will we kill one?" Mukje asks. "Who is strong enough to throw a harpoon accurately?" "We don't need harpoons," I say. "We have the Cossack muskets. They will kill the walrus by magic." We go down to the beach and put our biggest hunting canoe into the water, but the effort has left Mukje panting and

[119]

coughing, and he falls to the ground. "I have decided not to go," he says. We carry him back up to the house, and he wishes us good hunting, and we go. We paddle for a very long time out to sea, taking turns, because our bodies ache, and we are very tired. Then we come to the ice floes, and there are seven big walruses up on the ice. We go up very close. We can't stop coughing. The walruses are suspicious, but don't think we are close enough to dart our harpoons. We have a surprise for them. We come up to the first, and I shoot it in the head. Great amounts of blood come out of its head, and it roars and rolls over on its back and slides into the sea and sinks. We come up on the rest, which are very excited, but still are not diving into the water, and one by one we shoot all seven. It is very good hunting. They all fall into the water and sink. It is more walruses than we have ever killed before in one day, and we feel very proud. And there was no effort to it, and we did it very quickly.

We are very tired nonetheless, and paddle back slowly, with much resting. The sun is on the horizon when we get back to the village. I go in to see Mukje, who looks very weak. "Good hunting!" I shout. His face brightens. "What did you get?" he asks. "Seven walrus, Mukje, seven giants with long tusks." "That is very good news indeed," Mukje says. "I fancy a big walrus steak right now." "There is no steak, Mukje," I say, "only a scrap of rotten seal meat." "Why is there no steak?" he asks, puzzled. "They all sank in the sea," I tell him. "They all sank?" he says, a little disappointed. "Yes, Mukje, but such good hunting! Seven in one day!" "Yes, that's very fine, I have to admit it," he says. He lies back down and closes his eyes.

*　*　*

J was now sharing the room with a casual fourteen-year-old, popping her gum and reading movie magazines, who had just

[120]

had her illegitimate child by Caesarian. The baby was going up for adoption, but while it was there the first couple of days, she had all her school friends in to see it, and they all thought it was *so* cute. The young girl's father was in one day with another man, who asked him "Well, how do you feel being a biological grandfather?" After a day, the girl was walking around, after three days the baby had been taken somewhere by the appropriate agency, and the girl had walked out and gone home.

J was still flat on her back in bed, if anything weaker, and more irritable, and more impatient of the I-V tubes, and catheter tubes, but was still unable to take much food, and still discharging great amounts of blood.

Now another woman, older this time, was sharing the room, having her fourth child by Caesarian. "Fred will never find this out," she confided to J, "but I told the doctor to tie off the tubes this time." This woman had the television on all day to watch the soap operas.

George now had the opportunity to put on a smock and hold the baby, who lifted his head and looked around quite alertly, already able to follow a finger moved in front of him. J let the baby nuzzle around at her nipples, though he couldn't get anything yet but colostrum. Mainly he was fed concentrated formula which he inhaled ravenously with a sound like water sucking out of a drain, pausing at long intervals for gasping breaths, then continuing, at the end belching resonantly. The woman in the next bed had a frail little girl who nursed soundlessly, then made a quiet little bup at the end.

Then *that* woman was walking about, taking solider foods, preparing to go home, and J was still hemorrhaging, and the doctors finally admitted they were a bit worried, and thought perhaps they had left a tiny piece of the placenta behind, and decided to do a D. and C. They were going to do it one evening after he left. Through it all J, who was having a lot of pain and discomfort, and was now in the worrisome situation of knowing the operation had not gone quite right, was very calm and steady.

Only, as he was leaving, she took his arm and made him promise that after the operation he would phone up and ask how she was.

He drove home slowly, putting off getting there, because he knew it would be even emptier and colder than usual. When he got there, he heated up a frozen dinner and ate it, and then did not even make the pretense of reading a book. He simply remained at the table, his thoughts drifting, but keeping any eye on the clock.

The D. and C. was scheduled to begin at 8:00. It shouldn't take long, but he thought he would wait until 10:00 to call. Perhaps by that time he would be able to talk to J herself. At 10:00 he put his hand on the phone, and suddenly realized it was ringing. He picked it up. It was a woman's voice, from the hospital, asking if he would give the doctors his permission, if they saw that it was necessary, to remove J's uterus. He said yes of course. The woman said, properly, he should sign a statement to this effect, but this was a bit of an emergency, so they would just take his verbal statement for now, but would he please sign the statement as soon as he came in. He said he of course would.

He got in his car and drove to the hospital.

* * *

[Many pages were missing from the beginning of these papers, and again towards the end they become scattered. This is the last note I have in Dr. Harris's hand, written at a time when they had already been locked in the pack ice for several months, and, with scurvy taking its toll, seemed to be losing their battle to last through the winter, in the hopes of returning the following summer to the Esquimo village.]

loss of *Life*, oweing, I must beleeve, purelie to Mr *Mountagues*, stubborneness, tho in fairness to that *Honest Man*, I think at the Last his *Intellectuals* was deteriorating. But as our *Boyes* dy'd of

Scurvie, ther *Teeth* all falln out, loosing the Use of ther *Limbs*, coverd with *soars*, in most desprit Payne, he insistid that the sovereign *Cure* was *Seel Oyl*, & dos't em ceeselesslie wth his wretchid *Elixir* till they Gaggd on 't; & become so adamant in his *Theorie*, that he took my counter- *Theorie* as an infringement on his *Command* of the *Shipp*, to the Poynt where, had we had *Fresh Victual* to spare, he wou'd ha' forbidd us to eat of't! But *Jemmie*, & *Davie*, & his *Womman*, was of my Side, tho' they had perforce to pretend to oppose me; & tho we coud do little to ayd the others, we made shift, wt such small *Game* as we took,— latterlie, onelie *Ravens*,—& wch I insistid they eat Raw on the Spott, so they had a Morsell at least of *Fresh*; & the proof was, we sufferd little, whylst the Rest dy'd in miserie abowte us. The *Capt.* was kep in his *Madnesse*, by the fact that wt his *Iron Constitution* he sufferd very little, wch he took as Proof of the efficacy of his *Oyl*. By now the *Capt* presidid o'er a *Charnel Howse* Shipp of Dedd & Dying, wt its *Timbers* stove by shifting Ice, & we concludid on a desprit expedient; wch was to sett out *Cross Countrie* for the *Indian Village*. We was at first afrayd to Broach this to Mr *Mountague*; but when wee did, the glitter seemd to cleer from his *Eys* a Moment, & hee took us each warmlie by the *Hand*, & wisht us *God Speed*, & give us 2 *Muskitts*, & *powder* & *shott*, & *bisketts*; & most surprising of all, when hee saw us packing our *Journals* to take, he give us extracts of the Shipps *Log*; so that if we succeedid & hee not, some *relict* of his Navigational discoveries shou'd remayne beehind him; & wee took leave of this brave & good if Misguydid *Man*, all wt *Teers* in our *Eys*, each kno'ing he wou'd ne'er see tother this side the *Vale*; ones position no more nor less desprit then tothers. Indeed our *Harts* misgave as we contemplatid the houling Wilderness of snow & Ice beefore us; & nothing pusht us on but the *Spectre* of slow Death & insanity beehind us.

No, one thing more pusht mee at leest: at the end of a long & use less if not positivly harmfull *Life*, I had done one *Single good Thing*, wch went some way tourds justifying all: by concluding

[123]

that *fresh Victual* was the *receit* agaynst *Scurvie*, I had direckly sav'd *Jemmies* & *Davies* lives; & now, coud we but reech the *Indian Village*, I coud put in the *Indians* keeping my *Notes* on this discoverie; wch, eventually coming to the Attention of the *Russians*, must at last be publisht in the *World* at large, wt a consequent saving of the lives of countless *Mariners*.

* * *

The doctor met him in the hallway.

"We scraped it, but couldn't stop the bleeding, so finally we had to take the whole uterus out. I'm terribly sorry."

"That's all right. How is she?"

"I think she'll be all right now. She's had a rocky time, two major surgeries in a row, and she was already very weak from losing blood. We're giving her blood now. But there was absolutely nothing else we could do. You see, it's an easy matter to tie off the arteries from the uterus and stop the bleeding, but then the organ is no longer fed, and it dies, so you can't leave it in there. But on the other hand you can't just let her go on bleeding. I'm going to do a biopsy. What I'm almost certain it was is a very rare condition where a microscopic piece of the placenta is actually embedded in the wall of the uterus, and until every bit of the placenta is out, the uterus can't contract to its proper size, and so the bleeding continues. But I can't tell you how sorry I am we had to do it. We haven't told your wife, and perhaps you could keep it from her until she's a bit stronger."

He realized finally, with relief, that the doctor was not worried about J, but rather was worried about how she would take the loss of her uterus, of her ability to have children. But they only meant to have this one child anyway, so, since it had to happen, it was, after the fact, more of a boon than anything else, meaning she did not have to continue taking the pill.

[124]

They let him go into the intensive care room. J was again hooked up to all her I-V and catheter tubes, and this time was getting a pint of blood as well.

"Hi, I'm Milly," the nurse said. She looked very competent and professional, and was there full-time to monitor J and an old man on the other side of the small room, who obviously had also just come out of an operation. He was moaning, and breathing with irregular gasps. It was just past midnight.

"How are you?" George said to J.

She took his hand.

"Can you stay with me now?" she said.

"Yes. Is it painful?"

"Yes," she said. "But mainly I just feel terrifically tired, like I'll never have any strength again. It's really too much effort to talk. But please don't leave."

"I won't. Don't talk. Sleep if you can."

"Did they take out the uterus?"

"Yes."

"I knew they would. They were trying so hard to avoid having to. Did you try to explain to them that it doesn't matter?"

"No. I didn't think they would understand."

"It was one thing I hoped I would do well, but I guess I'm one of those who wasn't meant to have babies."

"Well, what it means is, modern technology is not all bad. In the 18th century you would just have been another statistic."

"They said that because of the loss of blood and so on, I won't be strong enough to nurse him, so he'll have to go on formula. I probably never would have got any milk anyway."

But after about an hour, he could see her breasts swell up under her hospital gown, and then begin leaking and dripping through the material. She was sleeping, and he stood next to her with tears in his eyes, because he knew how badly she wanted to nurse her child. However, when she woke up a few minutes later, and noticed her milk, she only commented on it with interest, and went back to sleep.

[125]

* * *

[This in Davie's hand:]

Perhaps 't was just that we had put that mad & sad *Shipp* at last behind us, but tho' we was in so desprit a Pass, I felt a kind of spredding Happiness. The Main, I am sure, is that I had my young *Wife* back, & this reconcil'd me to all: but next was the fine Weather, for tho' the Dayes was but short, there was a kind of Twi Light on either Side, wch give us more travelling Tyme, & ther was ne'er Wind nor Clowd, but onelie perfec Still Dayes of Crystal purity; & finally my Happiness was that, wt all our Hardshipps in this Hard Country, *we was able to live in it*, & this not because we ws *Modern Man*, but the opposite; because we had give ourselfs up to a Waye of Life alreddy Old when our *Civilization* was Young, a Waye of Life all Sophistication & injinuity, tho' previously, in our Arrogance, we had call'd it *Primitive*; & 't is our Modern Curse to see all in terms of Time, as if Time made all better, brou't onelie improvement; but yet here *outside of Tyme* we saw all perfecklie accomodatid to the *Land*. In our long Monthes Ice Bound in the *Shipp*, *Debbie* had seen what we must do, & had onelie waitid the Proper Moment to tell me we Must leave over Land, but she had not been idel & dispairing wt the Rest, she had workt steaddily wt her ivori *Needels*, & mayde us all *Cloaths* proper to the Climat, of tightlie stitch *Skins* & *Furrs*, & then from the shou'der Bones of *Seels* had carv'd us, as 't were, *specktacles* to wear 'gainst the glare of the Ice; & then we sett out not o'er Land, as *we* wou'd ha' done, for she said at this Time of Yeer 't was but a barren Desart where we wou'd starve; but took us instedd acrost the *Sea* Ice, where there was *Seels* to Eat, having pickt the moment to Beginn when the Dayes was long enough to give us some Travelling Time, & was growing rapidlie longer as the new *Spring* approacht. Each Night, an howre before Light was gone, she stoppt us, & show'd us, wt a

Skill Pracktise soon gave us as well, how to use our *Knives* to build a small *Snow Howse*, wch kept us Snug & Warm tho' we strippt off our *Cloaths* (wch else would have meltid the snow & Ice off 'em, & got wet & unuseable, but wch we kep outside, so they retayn'd ther frozen cover, but was pliable underneath,) & in Tyme we cou'd build this *Howse* in less than an Howre.

Thou' there had been but little *Animal* Life abowte our founder'd *Shipp*, before many Dayes Journie, we beginn to find *Seels* plentifull at theire breathing Holes in the Ice, & wt *Debbie* to tell us the Method, we soon become adept at lying on the *Ground* like a sleeping *Seel* ourselfs, then moving up a few feet when the *Seel* we huntid took his short *cat* Nap, at last coming so cloas, I cou'd shoot it in the *Hedd*, & we all rush up befor 't cou'd thrash into the Water. So that for Myself, I wantid our *Tripp* to go forward forever, so much Joy ther was for me in the Present Moment; onelie that Dr *Harris* was not so Young as the Rest of us, & he was wearing Lean & Haggard, tho' *Jemmie* car'd for him Daye & Nigt wt grate tenderness. But he was buoy'd up wt a kind of Desprit intensity to reach the *Indian Village*, & this Objective carri'd him forewards.

From Ash's to Ash's we goe, quoath the *Buriall Service*, & from Charnel *Howse* to Charnel *Howse* we went, for we arriv'd at the *Village* to find onelie *Corses*, & those scatter'd by the wild *Beests*, & the Food *Stores*, badlie wantid by us, emptie, or broak into & stol'n, by the *Bears* & *Wolves* & other *vermin*, & maynlie by the *Dogs*, some of wch was still living Feral in the Neighbourhood. 't Was not starvation, wch *Debbie* says, is oft, in this Hard *Land*, the cause of Death of intire *Villages*. This we cou'd tell for many Raisons: 1st the *Dogs* was present, all of wch wou'd have been eat; 2d, they had not built theire winter Snow *Howses*, but had still been living in theire summer *Howses* of hides & sticks,—wich means they had all been dedd not long after we left em,—& Summer is a Tyme of Plentie, not of Starvation, & so theire was onelie one cause of Death, wch *Debby* call'd the *Rus-*

[127]

sian sickness, wch she said had, in the past, carri'd off whole *Villages*; but wch we cou'd not blame on the *Russians* this Time, for 't was some *Plague* of our own bringing, & I said to Dr *Harris*, I humblie own myself bestid, *Sir*, in the debayte we somtime had forewards: Whether our Modern Advancement bro't forward *Man* out of Darkness, as I formerlie argu'd, or onelie carri'd him farther away from his aboriginal perfecktions; as you argu'd. For here are these very Fine *People*, who had befrenddid us & Helpt us, & for whom we meant onelie the best, & we have brou't em all to Death; & indeed, 't is not *our* Inlightenment we have brou't *Them*, but rather, *theire* Skills, wch are teaching *Us* to Live this very Moment. And now I pause to Refleckt on 't, I wonder wt Dredd how many fine *peoples* in this *World* have we brou't the self-same *Plague* & destruction in our dementid & Arrogant desire to bring em improvement? What, after all, at very best, have we to offer these *peoples*, living happy & content, wt-out disease, wt-out War, wt-out greed; in theire Innocence, even wt-out Sin,—what have we to bring em, but this same disease, war, greed, & sin. *Nay, nay, Davie*, quoath Dr *Harris*, 't is indeed terrible to think what we have done here, & may well have done elsewhere, & I have argu'd in these very Words before, as you well know; but I have come on reflecktion to alter my vuw, to believe *history* is an inevitable *Force*, that 't is *Mans* destiny will-he nill-he to cover the *Earth*, that had we not brou't, all blamesslie of any intention, disease to these *People*, then the next *Shipp* to come wou'd have, for soon all *peoples* shall come together, & ther will be a mixing of *Disease*, no dou't, & *Culture*, till all is Naturaliz'd, for I have observ'd, when a disease is long in a partickular *Race*, they become impervious to 't; so just as we are not harm'd by the sickness we have brou't wch is so fatal to these, so the *Indians* that *Columbo*'s Saylors consortid wt are not discomfitted by the disease of *Venery* wch has carri'd off so many of our *People*. Nor indeed, for that matter, have we the *Royal* Patents on warfare & greed, for did we not see desprit homicidal war in the else Paradisal *Isle* of the *Woemmen*? & have we not seen

[128]

groat-pinching Greed in the alreddy welthy *Indians* we stay'd wt down the *Coast*? So if we examine the Evidence, what can we conclude but that *Man* is every where the Same, a mixture of Good & Bad; for even a *Shipp* Lode of *Men* as wholly Good as you, *Davey*, might by inadvertance bring a *Pestilence*, & even *Men* as wholly Bad as myself might be a humble Agent towards ridding the *World* of Pestilence; & as we travell o'er the Face of the *Earth*, bringing more & more *men* together, shall we not have the more Opportunities to learn by the powerfull force of Example & Observation, the meanness & foolishness of *Greed* in one *Place*, the Bewtie & beneficence of *generosity* & *hospitalitie* in tother, till, in the end War & Conquest, & Avarice & Vanity, shall slowlie Vanish from the *Earth*, whilst by slow increments, sickness & famine shall yeeld to advances in Kno'ledge?[18]

We had, however, little Liesure for *Discourse*, but had to settle how best to get our *Papers* back to *Civilization*, wt-out the wch, our long *Journie* wou'd have been to no Purpose. Our first tho't, was to remayne at the *Village* intill such Time as the *Russians* return'd, wch we suppos'd had been a regular occurrence, but then *Debby* tol'd us, that they had not been since she was a Little *Girl*, & indeed we had notic'd before, that she spoke but little *Russian*, nor had any of the younger *people* in the *Village* spoke any, so then we realiz'd, we must take steps to some how Rescue ourselv's. Well, *Debby* had a *Desseign*, wch, when she unfoldid it, fill'd me wt equal Parts Dispair & Elation, & also wt Pride &

---

[18]AH MI GUD DR   HOW TO MUCH TRU U SAI   George HOW DO U ANSER?   NOW FOR FAK WE NO MOR HAVE HUNGER EVERBODI FEEDED   NO MOR GREED EVERYBODI SHARE/SHARE   NO MOR WAR   EVERYBODI LUV/LUV   NO MOR BAD "dictator" GUV EVERBODI HIS OWN GUV   NO MOR "racism" "sexism"   EVERBODI 1 RACE 1 SEX   NO MOR SICK   "Pestilence" ALL BE CURED   (ONLI SICK WE NOT CURE BE CANCER FROM AIR PARTICULS NUKE PEACE CLICKS   BUT NO BODI CATCH THIS SICK BEFOR HE BE 50-55   NOW/ TIME VOLUNTARI GOODBI AT 42 CURE THIS)

[129]

Wonder at the Boldness of this tiny little *Person*, a meer 6 *Stone* in wait, barely having left her first *Child Hood*. She said, in the *Traditions* of her *People*, were *Stories* of those who had taken *Dog* Sledds, & journi'd *E* for a Journie of Severall Mos., intill they had come at the Last to a *grate Sea*. *Debby* said once when she was very Yong she had gone a Journie wt her *Family* to a large *Village* many many Dayes Travell to the E; that she thou't we could find agayne, & that some among these *People* wou'd accompany us, & show us the Waye, to the *grate eastern Sea*. We stay'd in the dismal Ghost *Village* for severall Dayes, having good hunting of *Seels*, & eating & gaining back our Strength, & preparing four our Journie, & catching the *Dogs*, & learning from *Debby* how to controll the *Sledds*. We packt 2 *Sledds* wt all our *Gear* & provisions, & *Jemmie* drove 1, wt Dr *Harris*, riding upon 't; & *Debby* & I took t'other, after *Debby* had said Good Bye to the *Ghosts* of her *Familie* & *Frends*, wt much yipping & Yowling of *Dogs*, we Sett out into the Trackless *Interior*.

En route: Pracktise has made us adept at handling of the *Doggs*, & once we lern'd theire separate *Charackters*, & lern'd to relax & work wt em, instedd of pulling agaynst em, we travell'd *Post* Haste, & did not grow so Tir'd, nor did the *Doggs*, wch pull'd wt a Will, & seem'd to injoy the acktion, wch so did we, travling wt grate exhilaration in bright Sun Shine acrost level Ice, & the fine Northern Stillness. At 1st we went severall daies along the Coast before coming to the proper *Area* to turn inland. The *Seels* was exceeding shy, but the grate *White Bears* was common, & tho' very salvage, knew not to Fear us, & lett us come up very cloas, where we dispatch't em wt our *Musketts*. The first *Bear* we kill'd thus, we Fedd part to the *Dogs*, & eat Part, & stor'd some *meat* on our *Sledds* for later Dayes. The 2d we shott, the *Dogs* refus'd to eat, tho' they was surely famisht; & this most exasperatid us; & then *Debby* too refus't it, saying if the *Doggs* refuse 't, it means the *Ghost* of some one in her *Village* is in 't, & to eat of it wou'd be *Cannibalism*. She said she thou't 't was her Maternal *Uncle*, wch

some thing in the way it walkt remindid her of when we 1st saw
't! We listend not to this foolishness, & eat Hartilie of 't ourselfs,
but after this we found other *Game* to eat, & after we turnd inland
there was no more *White Bears*, wch sav'd us a repetition of this
silly *Superstition*; in partickular we found a large Wooley horned
Beest, like an *Ox*, wch was easie to Hunt, as it stopp'd still when
we approch't it, & gather'd in a Defensive *Circle*, *Horns* out, wch
may have stood it in Stedd agaynst *Bears* & *Wolvs*, but cou'd not
help it agaynst our *Musketts*. At Nigt we stoppt & made our *Snow
Howses*, wch we did so swiftlie & easilie now, we made 2, 1 for Dr
Harris, & *Jemmie*, so I shou'd have t'other in privacie wt my
Bride. If 't was not for the Importance of our *papers*, I cou'd wish
this our *Journie* to go on for ever.

* * *

Davie, Jemmie, and Doctor were very sick, and could not
walk or stand very well, or hunt game. We got very hungry and
ate two dogs. I told Davie to show me how to use the musket, but
he thought I couldn't. We stayed in our snow houses and didn't
travel for a while. I said if we killed all our dogs for food, we
couldn't travel anymore. I said we should try to hunt some small
game. I made traps and caught some lemmings, but it wasn't
much. Davie showed me how to load the musket. I went out and
practiced shooting at a piece of skin. Pretty soon I could hit it.
Then I went out with it, and got a ptarmigan, an oldsquaw, and a
little white bird. I felt pretty good. We ate those, and next day I
went out and got a little white bird, a doodly bird, and two
oldsquaws. We ate these and I killed one more dog and fed it to
the other dogs. Then we all felt better and able to travel again.
We went a little way, and the weather turned bad. There were
bad winds and ice blew against us and stung us, and we couldn't
see. The dogs didn't want to travel in it. We looked for a shel-

tered place against a litle hillside to make our snow houses, and when we dug into the hillside, we found a cave with a big animal frozen in it from olden times. I said this is good luck because we can stay here until the weather is good, and eat this big animal until we feel stronger. I feel the ghost of this big animal very strongly in the cave. Davie says there are no ghosts, but he carries a big box full of the ghosts of his travels. We lived in the cave but covered the big animal with ice, because it will rot very quickly if it feels the air. We ate a little bit every day while the wind howled outside, but even so Doctor died and we carried him outside the cave and covered him with snow.

The weather is good again, but Davie and Jemmie are too sick to travel. I bring them fresh game with the musket. I am getting very good with it. But they cannot eat, and are very thin, and I think they will die very soon. Tomorrow I will put big bullets in the musket and go out with the dogs and see if I can kill a woolly ox. If I can, that means I can feed the dogs, and we can travel. When Davie and Jemmie die, I will travel by myself to the land of my relatives. It is not too far. When I get there I will have Davie's son, who will be a big chief.

* * *

George had now completed transcribing and arranging all but a few scraps of the journals. He remembered Camus saying that the only tragedy was the early death of a happy man, but at this distance the number of years Davie lived seemed unimportant. George himself read through Davie's journals not with a sense that he was reading tragedy, but rather he was elated at the richness and fulness of what Davie had had the good fortune to experience. Davie's only real regret might have been the loss of his papers, but now they were found. The detailed natural history notes and species lists in Latin George had put in a box and mailed off to the British Museum, with a letter explaining their significance. He received a courteous reply, saying the papers would be filed away, however lack of funds precluded their being translated, or any other action being taken with them at present. Closer to home, the museum had got a grant to cover the publication of the book, and with that and the essay on his vita, he had been offered a teaching job. It was a relief, of course, but it also meant this very happy period of freedom, his "poor-man's sabbatical," was coming to an end.

Oh well. It was early summer, and George, J, and two-month-old Davie had gone out on the San Juan Islands with a party from the university to read gull bands. They were spending the weekend at a house on one of the larger islands. The gull island was a half-mile long piece of rock about two miles offshore from this island. J wasn't going to go out to the rock because of the baby, but the morning dawned clear and windless, and the water flat calm, the barometer high and steady, and the day was too beautiful to resist. They went out in two small boats carrying their picnic, spotting scopes, cameras, and metal spikes topped by little numbered red flags to mark territories.

The water, as the sun rose, was full of tufted puffins with their gaudy parrot bills, and rhinoceros auklets, with their breeding plumes and horns. They stopped the boats, and the whole party watched through binoculars, as a pod of killer whales rolled on the far horizon.

There was only one spot on the small island where they could land, at one end where a forty-foot wide split in the rock made a small cove. They drew up the boats and made them fast, and carried their gear up to the top. J spread out a blanket on a grassy area, where she could stay with the baby. No gulls nested at this end of the rock, but two pairs of black oystercatchers had nests, and these comical and extraordinary creatures greeted them with loud piping calls. They were chicken sized birds, rich lustrous black, with long wedge-shaped brilliant scarlet bills, and long, drowned-earthworm-pink legs. George took several photographs of the birds with his long-lens camera, and then moved away from them so they could get back to their nests. On the sheer sides of the rock, pigeon guillemots nested in crevices, and George spent some time photographing these as well. They were as black as the oystercatchers, but with a blaze of white in the wing, and bright scarlet legs and webbed toes, and when they gave their funny whirring call, the insides of their mouths were equally scarlet. Also on the steep ledges, and keeping to the color scheme, were lustrous black pelagic cormorants, small, snaky sinuous necks, green eyes, a large patch of white on the flanks. They nested side by side and moved their medusa heads around until George went one step too close, they then sailed out over the water, leaving their long slender white eggs behind.

Everywhere around them was the loud calling of the gulls, and the birds themselves in wheeling flight. These were glaucous-winged gulls (GW's to the scientists), large snowy white birds, with pale gray back and wings, a large powerful hooked yellow bill. George and the others put on hardhats before entering the colony proper.

But there was a difference this year. In past years they had gone late in the season, when most of the gull chicks were well grown, in order to band them. The gulls' nests were generally in plain sight, in open places in the grass, but the moment the eggs hatch, the chicks run into the nearby low shrubbery and hide. Their protective coloring is excellent, so they are quite difficult to find for purposes of banding. And additionally, when the adult gulls have young, they can be quite fierce in their defense, divebombing the banders with their droppings, and deafening them with their screams, and finally banging the hardhats with their heavy bills or clawed feet. After seven or eight hours of the incessant din, the banders begin to hallucinate very human sounding words for the cries: "Look out! Look out! Go back! Go back! Murder! Murder!"

But this year they had come early in the season. The gulls were still sorting out territories and mates, egg laying had not begun, and as a consequence they were not so defensive, and nearly ignored the human intruders. A high percentage of the chicks had been banded on this island every year for the past ten years. Therefore a fair proportion of the adult gulls now had bands on their legs. Over the years this had yielded considerable information about longevity and seasonal distribution. The plan this year was to look for banded adult gulls that appeared to be on territory, to read their band numbers (this was not difficult; the gulls let them approach within thirty feet, and then they read the bands with their powerful telescopes zoomed up to 60x magnification), then to pound in a stake with a numbered red flag on it, in the center of the territory, and enter band number and flag number in a notebook, along with marking the position of the territory on a map of the island. This way over the years information could be gained on whether gulls returned to the same nesting territory year after year. They especially watched for territories where both members of a mated pair had bands, because with these they would be able to tell, in subsequent years, if gulls retained the same mates for life, or if they switched from year to year.

It was very pleasant work in the warm sunny day, surrounded by gulls courting and defending their territories from other gulls, each person alone and absorbed in covering his sector of the island, watching each gull to see if it had a band, then watching it to determine its territory, then approaching it to the point that it became slightly nervous, indicating it would fly if approached nearer, then reading the numbers on the part of the band closest to you, then walking in a slow circle around the gull until the numbers were read all the way around. It was like a game between you and the gull, for this one gull would realize it had been singled out, and would watch you narrowly, while the other gulls ignored you, and would quite maddeningly turn around to face you as you circled it, so that the same portion of the band would continue to be toward you, or it would be standing on the edge of a cliff, so that there was no way to get on the far side of it without going out into the water, so you would have to chase it up, then wait for it to return to its territory, and hope in its new position after returning, the band would have spun around to a new side. Sometimes after you had painstakingly read all but the final digit, the gull would get bored with the game, and fly off for its morning's fishing, and you wouldn't see it again. But in the main, you finally read the band, and then drove in your stake and flag and made the proper notations in your notebook, and you worked with a slight urgency because, though no one would admit to it, there was a competition to see who would read the most bands.

At lunch time he sat slightly apart with J and the baby.

"How's it going?" J said.

"Well," he hedged, "just reading the bands is supplying lots of information."

"You don't think marking the territories is going to work?"

"Not the way we're doing it. The gulls are instantly responding to the red flags. They immediately rip them off the stake then scatter the pieces."

"Oh dear. Have you said anything to the others?"

"No, they'll work it out soon enough, and anyway, we're all enjoying ourselves so much it would be a shame to spoil it. To tell the truth, I find myself approaching the bird, and instead of checking numbers, I just think, Look how beautiful that bird is. The immediate experience, not what it may lead to."

"Is that what you think about when you look at me, my immediate beauty?"

"No, in your case, I still think about what it may lead to in another minute."

EPILOGUE

[Almost by chance I found, in the margin of one sheet of Latin scientific notes, a brief almost indecipherable message scrawled in an unsteady hand (still recognizably Davie's) which at first merely puzzled me, but which I am now convinced was the final communication from the party, written shortly before their death in the cave. What I like particularly about it is that it seems to be addressed to me, as the finder of the papers.]

Now more than e'er I am convinc't in the Goodnesse & Valew of my Life & of all Life. Please [see?] that thes Papers [several words smudged], Good Bye & *Amen!*

[Goodbye and Amen, Davie.][19]

[19]AN NOW "addressed" TO I   I TO MUCH LISTEN Davie   I TO MUCH
LISTEN   George
GOODBI

Flatiron Book Distributors Inc., 175 Fifth Avenue (Suite 814), NYC 10010